DAMSEL IN DISTRESS
THE HIDDEN REALM
BOOK TWO

D.N. HOXA

ALSO BY D.N. HOXA

The Reign of Dragons Series (Completed)

King of Air

Guardian of Earth

Warden of Water

Queen of Fire

The Pixie Pink Series (Completed)

Werewolves Like Pink Too

Pixies Might Like Claws

Silly Sealed Fates

The New York Shade Series (Completed)

Magic Thief

Stolen Magic

Immoral Magic

Alpha Magic

The New Orleans Shade Series (Completed)

Pain Seeker

Death Spell

Twisted Fate

Battle of Light

The Dark Shade Series (Completed)

Shadow Born

Broken Magic

Dark Shade

Smoke & Ashes Series (Completed)

Firestorm

Ghost City

Witchy Business

Wings of Fire

Winter Wayne Series (Completed)

Bone Witch

Bone Coven

Bone Magic

Bone Spell

Bone Prison

Bone Fairy

Scarlet Jones Series (Completed)

Storm Witch

Storm Power

Storm Legacy

Storm Secrets

Storm Vengeance

Storm Dragon

Victoria Brigham Series (Completed)

Wolf Witch

Wolf Uncovered

Wolf Unleashed

Wolf's Rise

The Marked Series (Completed)

Blood and Fire

Deadly Secrets

Death Marked

Starlight Series (Completed)

Assassin

Villain

Sinner

Savior

Morta Fox Series (Completed)

Heartbeat

Reclaimed

Unchanged

This book is a work of fiction. Names, characters, businesses, organizations, places, events, and incidents either are the product of the author's imagination or are used fictitiously. Any resemblance to actual persons, living or dead, events, or locales is entirely coincidental.

Copyright © 2023 by D.N. Hoxa

This book is protected under the copyright laws of the United States of America. Any reproduction or other unauthorized use of the material or artwork herein is prohibited.

CHAPTER ONE

Ax Creed

Too many trees. Too many scents. Way too many eyes on me as I went through the woods. The animals stayed away, though. Their instincts were much sharper than those of humans. Almost as sharp as a vampire's.

But I still had to keep reminding myself that it was almost over.

When we crossed into the Hidden Realm, and the magic shielding it from the rest of the world made the air heavy, one of the gates was halfway open, and eleven vampires were waiting for us.

It was important that I didn't lose it yet. I gave my word. I was going to keep it, no matter what.

Marie and Marcus were right behind me, their bodies shaking, their hearts beating like drums in my ears. The scent of their fear overpowered that of the woods and the animals and the vampires instantly. They'd seen the gates, too—and the vampires waiting for us. Five of the Sangria coven; another six from Redwood.

They siblings stayed close to me as we crossed through the gate and were finally inside the large walls that made the Hidden Realm.

Home.

Except right now, it felt just as foreign a place to me as the rest of the world.

I stopped in front of the vampires for a moment. The Sangria soldiers were ones I recognized. And I knew Ivan Petrov, too. The Redwood army commander. The woman standing next to him was a smaller version of him with long hair, and the four soldiers at their back had their hands on their swords already.

"Where...where is she?"

My eyes stopped on the woman standing next to the Redwood commander. Her hands were shaking. I didn't see as well in daylight, though the large trees to our sides shaded us perfectly, but I could make out the tears in her eyes just fine. She took a step closer to me before Ivan grabbed her by the arm.

"Where is Nikki?!" she demanded, her voice high-pitched, her wide eyes *begging* me.

"Nikki is gone," I forced myself to say. "She didn't make it."

Such simple words. My voice was ice-cold, too. No emotion. Nothing even remotely close to describing what those fucking words meant.

The woman screamed. She jerked her arm away from Ivan's hold, and a blink later, she was in front of me, slamming her fists on my chest. She was much stronger than she looked, but I didn't stop her. The pain felt mighty fine. It was a distraction. And even though she didn't hold back, and her strength shook me to my core, it was *nothing* compared to what the inside of my chest looked like.

It lasted barely a couple of seconds before Ivan grabbed her by the arms and pulled her back. His heart was hammering, too. He was trying almost as hard as me to control himself, his brown eyes full of hatred as they took me in, all the blood and the wounds and the torn clothes on my body.

That felt great, too.

The woman was sobbing, her shoulders shaking as she hid her face behind her hands. It distracted me, until Ivan moved again. He looked behind me, at Marie and Marcus, and he made to grab them when I was standing right there.

He must have lost his fucking mind.

I grabbed his wrist as soon as he raised his hand. I squeezed until I heard his bone cracking.

He didn't flinch, didn't make a single sound. Maybe he enjoyed the pain, too.

Attack me, I begged him with my mind. *Just give me something to do*.

He held my eyes instead. "You brought them here. Now we do the rest," he said, his voice perfectly composed, as you would expect from a commander.

Any other day, I'd have laughed in his face.

"You touch them, you die."

The soldiers behind him unsheathed their swords, and the Sangria ones did the same. I didn't let go of Ivan's wrist, and he didn't move away for a long second. I'd never wanted a fight so badly in my life. It didn't matter that the sun was up, and I was starved for blood, had wounds all over my body—I wanted to fight. If he could just attack me. If he could just take my fucking mind off *everything*, just a for a moment...

Ivan stepped back, teeth gritted. I had no choice but to let him go. Fucking pussy.

I started walking ahead, the sobs of the woman still echoing in my ears. We had to walk another five minutes on foot to get to the road. The soldiers were behind us. Redwood followed, too.

The heat was almost making me dizzy. I was wounded, though not bleeding anymore, the sun was shining, and my insides had all but melted. Thoughts spun in my head so fast, it was a miracle I could keep my fucking balance.

Nikki is gone. And I was still here.

By the time we made it to the road and the SUVs, I had no chance of keeping my fangs on the inside. One of the soldiers started walking around the car, the keys in his hands. Before he could reach the driver's door, I grabbed his arm and took the keys from him. Nobody was riding with us.

"Get in," I told the siblings, opening the back door for them, and they didn't hesitate. The soldiers waited until I turned the ignition on and started driving before they got in the other SUV. Behind them, the Redwoods were still watching, Ivan with his phone pressed to his ear. I kept my eyes on him through the rearview mirror until I took the U-turn and lost sight of him. Just my luck that he was able to control himself when he wanted to do nothing more than rip my throat out. I wished he'd fucking tried.

It was another ten-minute drive to the Sangria castle. I made it in front of the gates in five. The roads were clear, no vampires in sight at this time of day. Nothing standing in my way.

The siblings sat in the back, holding hands with each other, hearts still beating a mile a minute, but they never made a single sound. The scent of their fear kept me company until I was inside the castle gates. I parked the car right there and left the keys in the ignition. Somebody would take it to the garage.

"Stay close," I told them when we got out of the car. The castle yard was silent, not a soul in sight, but I was sure someone inside would be awake. Definitely Robert. He always waited up for me when I returned from the outside world.

And as soon as I stepped on the first marble stair of the castle's main entrance, the double doors pulled open from the inside.

Ten soldiers were in the hallway, waiting. I didn't think I'd ever seen that many vampires awake in daylight in all the years I'd been turned. They all looked miserable as fuck to be there, too.

"If you would follow me, sir," one of the soldiers said, keeping a good distance from me. They all did, just like always. I liked my personal space, but fuck if I didn't wish one of them would give me a reason right now. If they didn't, I was afraid I was going to fucking explode soon.

But nobody came close to me. The soldier didn't wait for a reply. He turned around and started walking deeper into the castle while the others watched. I followed, hands fisted tightly, no longer even trying to retreat my fangs. I didn't have the energy to waste.

The soldier led us down the marble hallway to the right of the main room, and straight to the back of the castle. After we went through the third set of doors, I knew exactly where we were going. The basement on this side of the castle was for Robert. He kept his precious books and wines down there, and it was as far away from the sun as one could get in this castle. More soldiers were awake—a lot more than I thought. We passed another fifteen, and none of them looked at me. They just kept guard by the walls, as if Robert was getting ready for a fucking war.

My unease grew with every step I took. How long until I could no longer control myself? I'd lost blood. I was craving it. I'd never been this close to losing it in a long time.

When we reached the second level underground, there were two more soldiers in front of the large wooden doors waiting for us. The one who led us there stepped aside and let us through.

"Why is everybody afraid of you?" the boy behind me whispered so low, I barely caught it. I kept my eyes on the soldiers pulling the doors open.

A second ticked by.

"Should *we* be, too?"

So much fear in his voice alone.

I forced myself to turn around and face the siblings. Not a drop of blood left in their faces. They were worse off than me, scared out of their minds. Of course, they would be—they didn't belong here. All of this was brand new to them, and the castle and the vampire soldiers surrounding them could be too much for anyone, let alone sorcerers.

Taking in a deep breath, I looked at the boy. "I made a promise, kid," I said as calmly as I could muster. "I'm going to keep it. As long as I'm here, you'll be safe."

The boy didn't believe me. The woman cried silent tears but no sound escaped her. That was the best I could give them right now, so I turned around again. The doors were wide open, and Robert was standing in the middle of his cellar with his hands folded in front of him.

He wasn't the only one. Abraham Jones and Curt Vanner were with him, just a couple of feet away. And they were all watching me.

So much power inside one room. Out of the three of

them, Vanner was the youngest at a hundred and ten years old. Jones was the oldest, the most powerful. And the way he looked at me right now said he wanted me dead already.

Now, *he* would be a worthy opponent. If I picked a fight with him, I wouldn't even be a hundred percent sure I'd survive it, which made the idea all the more exciting. But, unfortunately, this was the man who found Damsel when she was a kid, took her in, looked after her. I would not be picking a fight with him today...unless *he* wanted to.

"Axel," Robert said with a nod when I stopped three feet away from them, his eyes already behind me, on the siblings still shaking as they held onto each other.

"Did you kill her?"

The words rang in my ears like bells. I looked at Abraham Jones, his pitch-black eyes, the thin line of his lips. His hands were fisted, the air around him heavy as if his pores were leaking magic.

"Jones," Robert warned, but the man didn't even look at him. He stepped forward instead, holding my eyes, jaws locked.

I looked away. It cost me, but unless he provoked me...

"Look me in the eye and tell me the truth," Jones said, his voice now barely a whisper. "Did you kill Nicole?"

I didn't remember moving, but I was in front of him before I could blink, eyes on his, just like he asked. My fingernails dug into my palms and I did my best to keep my face expressionless, but it wasn't working. Abraham Jones wasn't surprised. He didn't bat an eye at finding me in front of him so suddenly.

He should have, if he had the balls to fucking *accuse* me. Not only that, but he'd already made up his mind about it. All he wanted was for me to admit it.

Robert was beside us the next second. "We agreed on

this, Abraham. The sorcerer is here. There will be no questions—"

"No," I spit, and it was all I could do to keep from growling. "I did not kill her."

The man was suddenly shocked. His eyes widened and his lips parted because he could see it in my eyes. He could smell it on my skin. He knew truths from lies, probably better than most. And this truth was undeniable. I didn't kill Damsel. I would have burned the whole fucking world to save her. If I'd only been a little faster...

"Who did?" Jones whispered, stepping back, the image of the monster he truly was now hidden behind his pain.

"Abraham," Robert warned again, but I didn't mind. It was already done.

"Jacob Thorne and his minions," I told him, and his eyes changed yet again. His heart picked up the beating, too, just as loud as those of the siblings behind me. He looked so fucking murderous for a moment, it was like a knife twisting in my gut. The pain and the need for revenge I saw in him was undeniable. He'd really cared about Damsel.

"Jacob Thorne couldn't have killed her," he finally said, but he didn't sound very sure.

"He did. Even after she let it all go, he did. They trapped her in a hole in the ground, buried her under an entire fucking house, then set the pieces on fire." I looked down at my hands, at my burned skin that had already started to heal. It no longer even hurt. Or maybe I just didn't feel it. "He died with her." Which was how I knew that he was the luckiest bastard in the fucking world. If he'd been alive...my gods, if he'd been alive, I'd have had the patience of a thousand worlds with him. I'd have kept him with me for decades.

Jones's eyes were on my hands, too, before he lowered

his head for a moment and composed himself. He cared about Damsel, but he also was the ruler of his coven. He had business to get to—the same business that had gotten Damsel killed.

I didn't regret it, though. If it wasn't for it, I would have never met her. I would never even know she existed.

"Is this her?" Curt Vanner said, looking behind me, his brown eyes glossy as if he were holding back tears. "And what is *he* doing here?"

"I gave you the order, Axel," Robert said next. "You should have left the boy behind."

"Well, I didn't," I said. "He stays."

"He's a sorcerer. It's impossible—" he started, and I had a lot of respect for Robert. Not only because he saved my life and turned me himself, but because of everything he'd done for his coven since I remembered. He took care of his people. And I appreciated that.

But I was not in the right mindset right now, and he needed to know it before things got out of hand.

"Then you *make* it possible," I said through gritted teeth. "He stays."

Robert wanted to argue. It's what we always did. But he must have seen something in my eyes. He must have sensed something with his instincts because he clamped his mouth shut and nodded.

"We will need the sorceress to follow us." He turned to the side, his eyes on Marie next.

"Then lead the way."

"Not you," Robert said, and I smiled again.

"If I'm not going, they're not going." That should have been clear to them by now.

Suddenly, Robert was in front of me, hands on my

shoulders as if he wanted to *hug* me before he whispered in my ear: "What the fuck is the matter with you?"

I put my hand on his chest and pushed him away.

"Where they go, I go." If they wanted to fight me about it, I was right there. I was *begging* them for it, too. *Just put me out of my fucking misery already.*

"Let him," Jones said from our side. "We've wasted enough time." And he turned around, going deeper into the cellar where there were no lamps on the walls. All I could see was a wide hallway with metal doors to the sides.

Curt Vanner followed, but Robert didn't move away from in front of me. The way he watched me...I'd never seen that look in his eyes before. Then again, we'd never been in this position before, either. The shit he did was never personal with me, not like now.

"Remember yourself, Axel Creed," he whispered and let that sink in for a minute, holding my eyes. He didn't wait for a reply before he turned to follow Jones and Vanner.

Gritting my teeth, I raised my chin. Robert was just as big a monster as me. If I ever laid a hand on him, or he on me, one of us would end up dead, I had no doubt about that. I'd never even entertained the idea before, but I had never been in these shoes, either.

Still, I wasn't afraid, not in the least. He had shit to lose. I didn't. Not anymore.

I turned to the siblings as if to make sure they were still there, though their heartbeats were in my head. Marie was no longer crying, and the boy didn't look as pale as minutes ago. Not that it mattered. They were here for a reason, and I couldn't stop Robert, or even Jones, from getting to them. The best I could do was be in it with them.

So, I followed after the men, and the siblings came after me, slowly, dragging their feet. There was a turn to the left of the hallway I hadn't even noticed. The darkness wasn't an issue for us—except the kid, but his sister was guiding him. And the men had stopped at the very end of the narrow hallway, in front of a large door made of metal, waiting for us.

And the closer to it I got, the more I smelled the air.

Smelled the magic.

I stopped dead in my tracks, confused for a minute. I sniffed hard, sure that I'd smelled it all wrong.

It was there, though. The scent of magic hanging in the air was unmistakable. It was raw, spicy, the kind that stuck to big groups of sorcerers, invading the air, sticking to my nostrils.

"What is this?" I asked Robert, but he barely even looked at me. He instead turned to the door, pressing his palm on the metal for a moment, and another wave of magic released from it.

Robert stepped back, shoulders rigid, and he took a moment before he grabbed the handle.

Then he opened the door.

CHAPTER
TWO

At least a hundred candles burned to the right of the room, placed on the hardwood floor, on the dressers next to the walls, as well as on a few golden candle holders. Their orange light was warm, and the lamps opposite them spilled light of the same color. The room was large, twice the size of mine, and it had a door on the far right wall, a small kitchen on the left corner...and an old woman was sitting on a rocking chair with a book in her hands, a pair of half-moon glasses barely holding onto the bridge of her nose.

She raised her head when the men walked in, and she stretched her lips as if she meant to smile. She closed her book and put it on the small table near her with two candles burning on it, waxed right to the tabletop. Her hair was a silver grey and tied behind her head. Her eyes were an icy blue that almost reminded me of Damsel's. The scent hanging about her was unmistakable, especially when I entered the room. The magic hanging onto her skin was the same as Marie's.

She was definitely a sorceress.

When she stood up from her chair, she was still smiling, taking her glasses off as she watched us.

"Good morning, gentlemen," she said, her voice soft and sweet.

"Good morning, Alida," Robert said with a nod. "You're already up."

"Oh, I haven't slept yet," she said. "That's what a good book will do to you."

I looked at Robert, at Jones, at Vanner.

"What the fuck is this?" Why was a sorceress locked up behind that door, behind all that magic, in Robert's fucking wine cellar?

"I'm glad you liked it," Robert said to her, like he hadn't heard me at all.

"I'm almost done with the ones you brought me last month," the woman said, her grey brows raised.

"Then I'll be sure to send new ones," Robert said.

Jones stepped forward. "Alida, if you please," he said, waving for her to approach, before he turned and looked behind me, at Marie.

And when Marie didn't move, he turned to me, looking me dead in the eye without a word.

Confused out of my fucking mind, I stepped aside and raised my hand toward Marie. She hesitated, and it took her a good few seconds to make up her mind about it, but she finally grabbed it. Her skin was ice-cold, palm sweaty.

"Oh, my. Who is that?" the sorceress said, offering a real smile as she took in Marie.

"We're hoping you can tell us that," Robert said, and with Marie's hand in mine, I slowly stepped closer to the sorceress.

"We shall see," the sorceress said. She came closer,

searching Marie's face, her hair, her clothes. "Come close, child." And she raised her hands toward her.

Marie didn't look at me. She just let go of my hand and went to the woman, putting her hands on hers without the slightest hesitation.

"Are you...are you Alida Morgans?" Marie said in a shaky whisper.

The woman's face broke into a wide smile, showing all of her yellowed teeth. "Why, yes, I am," she said. "It's good to meet you, Marie."

"But...but..." Marie started, shaking her head, like she couldn't find the words to speak.

The woman laughed a bit. "Hold on, darling. This won't be long," she whispered, and closing her eyes, she breathed in deeply.

Magic sizzled in the air. I was a second away from grabbing Marie and pulling her back. I had no clue what the fuck was happening, but this didn't seem right. None of this made any fucking sense.

But before I could move, the sorceress opened her eyes again, a wide smile stretching her wrinkled face.

"Is it her?" Jones asked in half a voice.

She nodded. "It is."

I STEPPED in front of Robert before we turned the corner to go back to the wine cellar. Jones and Vanner were ahead. Marie and Marcus were behind me still. They stopped when I did.

"Move," Robert spit, but I wasn't planning to.

"What the fuck is this, Robert? Who is that?" I nodded

back at the end of the narrow hallway, to the room with the sorceress still in it.

"None of your business," Robert said.

"I've made it my damn business."

"You're crossing lines, Axel. Remember your place," he repeated.

Well, since he went there... "You crossed plenty of lines when you lied to my fucking face and sent me out there. What—you didn't think I would be back here asking for answers?" I stepped closer to him. "Or maybe you just hoped I *wouldn't* be back at all?"

"For fuck's sake," he said, like what I suggested was plain ridiculous to him. "This is stupid. We're better than this. We're friends—"

"Oh, yeah? Were we friends when you kept this fucking secret from me?" *Friends,* like the word even meant something to him. Or me. "What the hell is the meaning of this?" I pointed toward the end of the hallway, and he knew exactly what I was asking. "You kidnapped a fucking sorceress and kept her here for...how long exactly?"

"We didn't kidnap her," he said, then flinched. "Technically. She chose to be here." I raised a brow. Did he really expect me to believe that? Why in the world would a sorceress *choose* to be in a place her kind designed for their sworn enemies? "Look, we needed her. We needed to see what was out there."

"See how?"

"She's a seer. She's not powerful, simply gifted. She tells us things sometimes." It cost him to say every single word, but that didn't mean I wasn't going to make him say more.

"A seer," I whispered. "She told you about Marie."

"She did."

My hands fisted tightly. "Did she know what was going

to happen?" Did that woman actually know that Damsel was going to die?

"No, that's not how it works. All she could give us was an address—that's it."

A long breath left me. "Why? What is Marie? She's been touched, hasn't she? Not a real vampire."

Robert held my eyes for a second. It was the first time since I'd met him that he looked afraid. It made me more uncomfortable than anything else. Robert Sangria was not easy to scare.

"Go to bed, Ax. We'll talk more at nightfall," he said, and he stepped aside to walk away lightning fast, as if he was afraid I'd stop him again.

But I wouldn't. As much as I hated it, I needed to lie down. I needed blood. I needed to *think*. And Marie and her brother needed beds, too.

They were no longer shaking, but they were far from comfortable. I didn't need to say anything—they knew to follow me when I made for the door. They would stay in my house, which I'd built behind the castle. It would be safe. Nobody had ever dared to come close to it, and it was still daylight. At least for the next few hours, I wouldn't have to worry about their safety too much.

OVER AN HOUR UNTIL SUNDOWN.

My veins were full of blood, my wounds closed, though some scars and some bruises remained. After putting the siblings in a guest room down the hallway from mine, I showered and lay down, too. I didn't move at all for six hours.

But my mind never shut down.

I'd slept that day. When Damsel stayed with me, I'd slept, and I hadn't even noticed myself drifting away. I thought I would today, too. I was exhausted. Had lost a lot of blood. Had had my fucking soul ripped right out of me. But I couldn't even keep my eyes closed for more than a few minutes at a time because all I saw was her. That fire. All I could imagine was her—*burning*.

By the time I made the decision to leave my room, everything in it except the bed was in pieces.

My time would come. They would *all* burn, too. I'd make damn sure of it.

Right now, I still had a promise to keep, and as much as I didn't want to even think about it, I had to. The siblings were my responsibility now, and we were in a city swarming with vampires. If there's one thing this life had taught me over and over again, it was that vampires can't be trusted. Not even those who call you their *friend*. Secrets are everywhere. Most people didn't have the balls to be who they were, reveal their true face to the world, so they acted behind people's backs to avoid the consequences. Sneaky fucking bastards. I'd be stupid to trust anyone here —including Robert.

Definitely stupid to trust a sorceress who'd *wanted* to live locked under a fucking castle in the Hidden Realm, but there was one thing I could trust without a doubt: magic. It didn't have a mind of its own. It couldn't betray you or change its mind or wear two faces. It did what it was meant to do, and that was that.

So, I stopped by the door of the guest room and listened to the heartbeats of the siblings. Steady, their breathing even. They were asleep. I could count on the sun to keep vampires away—and the fact that besides the rulers and the guards who'd seen me, nobody else knew the siblings were here yet. I only had an hour to get back, and I planned to be here when night fell.

That's why I ran at my full speed outside my house and into the castle. No more guards by the doors or in the hallways, just like I'd hoped. Not that anybody would have stopped me—or tried to, anyway. But I'd rather nobody knew about this at all. The sun usually made me uncomfortable. Not this time. I felt like a stranger wrapped up in old skin already. Maybe that's why I didn't even feel the sun anymore.

Three minutes later, I was in Robert's wine cellar, walking down the dark hallway. The magic in the air almost suffocated me. You couldn't feel it at all until you were five feet away from the large metal door. I had to hold my breath when I stopped in front of it just to give myself time to adjust.

Robert had simply put his hand on the metal to release the magic. I tried to do the same, but as soon as my fingertips touched the ward, my skin burned. No problem, though. I could break the door down. It would take a while to get through the magic, but it could be done. The pain of the burns would be welcome, too.

But I never had to even raise my hands.

The moment the magic released in the air, it was much easier to breathe. It felt like an invisible weight lifted from my shoulders, and then the handle of the door turned from the other side. I heard the metal groaning and smelled the scent of the sorceress as soon as the door pushed open just a tiny bit.

The sight of her icy eyes almost startled me when I stepped to the side, though I'd expected her to be there.

I managed my body perfectly fine most of the time. Having enhanced hearing was great—except when everybody else around you shared it. It was important to keep your breathing in check, your heartbeat steady, your emotions perfectly masked. It had taken a lot of years and a lot of practice, but I never slipped—*never*, until Damsel. She had a way of playing with my body and my mind any way she pleased.

Nobody else, though. This sorceress wouldn't be able to hear my heartbeat, but I still kept it under control. It had become an instinct by now. And when she saw my face, she pushed the door open all the way.

"Hello," she said, her voice soft, barely a whisper. If I'd ever imagined as a kid how a grandmother would sound, it was probably this.

"I need your help," I told her. Not my favorite words in the world, but things were what they were, and my choices were limited.

The sorceress raised her grey brows for a moment, then stepped aside so I could walk in. There wasn't much she could do to me in there without my knowing about it. I felt every small change in the air, especially in closed spaces like this, so I wasn't afraid. But I was nervous still.

I closed the door behind me, and the sorceress moved back a couple of feet. It made me feel more at ease, too, even though she was smiling.

"And who are you, young man?"

"I'm Ax," I said. "I brought back Marie and her brother."

"Oh, yes, I remember," she said with a nod. "How are they?" Her hands were folded in front of her. She didn't look like she was even a little bit afraid, which kept me a bit on edge.

"Safe," I said, keeping my focus on the room, too. There was nobody here with us, but magic could be sneaky. And invisible. I'd witnessed it firsthand when fighting Jacob Thorne. "But they won't be for long."

"No, I suppose they won't," she said, her smile vanishing as she turned around and went deeper into the room, all the way to her rocking chair, but she didn't sit. She sat in her rocking chair with an exhausted sigh, like she was barely keeping herself up.

"I need your help," I repeated, following her but keeping a good distance between us. "I need magic that will keep other vampires away from them."

The woman wasn't surprised in the least. "Ax, was it?" she said but didn't wait for an answer. "What are they to you?"

"Nothing." That's what they were. "But I made a promise to keep them safe."

"And you alone are not enough." She said it like she knew it for a fact.

"I am, actually." Except I didn't plan to be in the Hidden Realm for long. I still had people I could trust for a little while here, but vampires could be killed by other vampires. Magic, on the other hand, was different. "I'm most concerned about the boy. The woman has fangs. She can move fast. She can get away. The boy can't." And he was way too young to have magic strong enough to keep himself safe.

"I see," the woman said with a nod, then suddenly raised her hand toward me. "May I?"

Goose bumps raised on my arms. She was a fucking sorceress, too, same as the people who had taken Damsel from me. The desire to bite her head off before she even realized what was happening was strong, but I resisted because I needed her. Right now, I needed her.

"What is she?" I asked her instead. She lowered her

hand to her lap again, still not surprised. She hadn't *really* expected me to willingly touch her. "What did you see? Why did you tell them about her?"

"I'm afraid it's complicated and not my place to share."

I laughed. "You're a sorceress who somehow lives under a castle inside the Hidden Realm. That's complicated, too, but I'll pretend I understand it." I took a step closer. "What is Marie?"

The woman lowered her eyes to her lap—not afraid exactly. Just…confused. "She's been touched by a Vein spirit."

"Yes, I know that. But why is she here?" There were plenty of sorcerers out there who were touched. Damsel was, too. At least that was the only explanation after what I'd seen, even though it made absolutely no fucking sense. Vampires and Vein magic didn't mix—but what the hell did I even know about that?

The woman pressed her lips together but didn't speak.

"Just tell me. If I don't know, I can't keep her safe." She must have cared. People cared about this shit—they were the same kind, weren't they?

"It is not your place to keep her safe. Nobody is safe," she finally whispered. If my hearing wasn't what it was, I would have been sure I heard her wrong. "I can help you with a ward for them. I will need until tomorrow, though. I need my sleep. At this age, there's only so much energy you can spend." She smiled again when she looked at me.

"They will kill her. If they get their hands on her, they will kill her." Or do something even worse than those sorcerers who'd locked her in that basement. This woman had to know that.

"They will not hurt her," she said instead, and she sounded so sure I was tempted to believe her. When she stood up, the urge to step back was ridiculous, so I didn't move an inch. And again, she reached out her hand toward me. "May I?"

I ignored her just as well as the first time.

"How would you know that they won't hurt her?"

"Because they need her," she said without missing a beat.

"*Why?*" I knew they needed her. That's why Robert sent me out there. That's why Jones sent Damsel out there.

"I'm afraid I can't tell you that," she said, shaking her head like she was *sorry* for me.

I only had so much patience. If I stayed here longer, I knew I would push too hard, and I still needed her for the siblings. Closing my eyes for a second, I breathed deeply. I would be back tomorrow, try again. And if she still refused to tell me, I could always push Robert as far as he could be pushed.

So, I turned to leave, except...

"All is not lost."

I stopped. I turned. The sorceress stood there, hands folded in front of her, looking like a loving grandmother for real now, instead of what she truly was. She held my eyes, never even blinking, and when I stopped in front of her, she had her hand outstretched again, asking for mine.

"What did you just say?"

She looked down at her hand instead. "May I?"

Fucking hell, it was all I could do to keep my fangs from coming out. What the fuck was it about her?

The temptation was too much. Before I even realized it, I raised my hand and put it in hers. I must have been out of my fucking mind. And the moment our palms touched, the sorceress closed her eyes and let go of a deep breath, like she'd been waiting a lifetime to hold my fucking hand.

The second lasted an eternity. I searched every inch of her face, every inch of her body, but I found nothing alarming. A little heat spilled from the palm of her hand into mine, but it wasn't uncomfortable. I could ignore it easily.

It occurred to me that I was making a big mistake touching her. Who knew how magic ever really worked? One could do all kinds of shit with it, especially if they drew blood.

But the sorceress didn't attack me. Instead, when she opened her eyes again, they were filled with tears.

I stepped back instantly.

"You poor soul," she breathed, bringing her hand to her chest. "You've suffered so much."

Oh, for fuck's sake.

What the hell was wrong with me? Did I really think that she'd have something useful to tell me because she asked to touch my hand? I was making an ass of myself.

"I'm fine, lady. You don't need to worry about me." I didn't need her fucking *sorry*. I didn't need anybody's *anything*. And I was going to turn to leave again, but...

"You and her both." My feet were glued to the floor instantly. "You share the same pain. The same damage. The same soul." Her voice was hushed, like she was afraid to speak the words out loud.

Before I knew it, I was in front of her again, looking down at her wide eyes. My heart was hammering, but I didn't care even if she could hear it because I knew who she was talking about. I knew what she meant, as absurd as it was.

"She's gone," I whispered, and if she didn't see the look in my eyes and know to *never* give me that bullshit again, she deserved what was coming for her.

But the sorceress smiled. "All is not lost," she repeated

and raised her hand again. Her fingertips barely grazed my stubble, but I didn't move away. "There's a saying among sorcerers. Those who walk their own path shall never be lost."

I returned the fucking smile. "You know what my path is, don't you? You know where it will lead me." Out there in the human world until every one of her kind was dead. She was a *seer*—that's what Robert had called her. What were the odds that she actually knew?

"Yes," the sorceress said. "But *you* don't."

My head moved to the side, and I held her eyes, sure she'd slip any second.

She didn't.

And I realized just how much power I'd given her since the second I touched her hand. Here I was, waiting for an answer from a stranger—worse, *a sorceress*, and I was ready to believe her, too.

I needed to get the fuck out of here asap. So, I stepped back.

"I'll be back tomorrow." Whatever magic she could give me to keep the siblings safe, I'd take it. Everything else was irrelevant...or so I thought.

But the door seemed like a mile away. My legs were heavy as if my own body wanted to drag me down. And I knew exactly why. As much as I didn't want to play these fucking mind games with this woman, I was too curious. Far too curious not to ask.

"How did you know?" I said when the door was already open. A single step and I'd be right outside.

"Know what?"

"That we have the same soul." I was sure she was talking about Damsel. She was the only one who'd awakened my mating instinct, the only woman I'd ever wanted to be mated to.

"Because I see it," she simply said.

That's how I knew she was full of shit. "She's dead." The words sounded bitter on my tongue. So fucking bitter, it was going to take the blood of every sorcerer out there to get rid of it, and I already couldn't wait to start.

"Her heart beats," the woman said, eyes closed for a second, as if she could *see* Damsel's heart right there behind her lids.

Her heart beats.

Hearts only beat when a body is alive.

I didn't remember myself moving, but the sorceress's arm was in my hand and I was suddenly towering over her again. She finally looked afraid. Terrified, even.

But I couldn't care less.

"She's alive?" Was that what she was saying?

And the woman nodded.

It felt like someone had poured lava all over me, but I didn't let go of her.

"If you're lying to me, I will fucking cut you to pieces." I said the words slowly so she wouldn't miss a single one.

But she still didn't speak. She didn't tell me that she wasn't lying—or that she was...and it didn't even matter. *Her heart beats.* Those words were enough. If there was a chance, even the smallest chance in the universe that she was right, I was going to find out. If Damsel was alive, I was going to search the whole fucking world until I found her, no matter how long it took.

"Where is she?" I demanded, and the sorceress was shaking now, though I couldn't feel her reaching for her magic at all. My fangs were out, and I had no care to control my expression anymore.

"I'm afraid I don't know that," she finally said.

I waited for her heart to skip a beat. I waited for any hint that she was lying through her teeth.

She wasn't—just like she hadn't been when she said that Damsel's heart still beat.

I let go of her and stepped back, feeling a million things at once. I snapped back into my own skin, just like that. The thirst for blood hadn't quenched, but...*all was not lost,* just like this woman said.

The view swam before my eyes when I made it to the door again.

"Walk your path," she whispered again as I pushed the door closed behind me.

I didn't turn. I didn't even look at her again. I didn't care what more she knew or what she didn't—there was a chance that Damsel was truly out there somewhere. That's all that mattered to me now.

And tomorrow, as soon as the old sorceress gave me the magic to keep the siblings safe, I'd be walking my fucking path right to her.

CHAPTER
THREE

Nikki Arella

I ALWAYS THOUGHT I could stay up during the day if needed, and I would handle it just fine. But it was one in the afternoon, and I hadn't slept in two days. I was so tired, I could barely get my body to move. Definitely not handling it as well as I thought I could, but...

"We're here."

I turned to Jacob Thorne, as if I was surprised to find him with me, the wheel in his hand. As if I hadn't been riding with him in his truck for the past five hours. In broad daylight.

Just that reality didn't feel all that real right now. What my memories of the night before were telling me was plain ridiculous, too. Nothing really made any sense to me.

And through all that chaos in my mind, Ax's words still spun in my head over and over again. *I will burn the whole fucking Realm to the ground, as long as you're with me.*

It wasn't just what he said. Not even that he meant it, and I believed it.

It was knowing that I would apparently do the same for him without hesitation that fucked me up like this.

And the fight, the monster that had come out of me, the green bubble of magic that had been wrapped around me when I woke up with Jacob Thorne, under the burning pieces of a ruined house...

The deal he'd offered. The deal I'd accepted. The way we'd gotten out of that hell, how long we'd had to walk, hiding from humans and sorcerers, until we got to his stupid red truck.

Every second since.

Fucked up. Plain ridiculous. *Unreal.*

But I had no idea that things were about to get even more absurd for me soon.

The wooden gates ahead weren't half as big as the gates of the Hidden Realm. All I could see behind them were trees. When Jacob had taken us through a woods down a narrow dirt road just off the highway somewhere in Minnesota, I thought for sure he'd made a wrong turn. But now, twenty minutes later, I realized he knew exactly where he was going.

"Wait here," he said before he got out of the truck, leaving the driver's door open and the ignition still on. Warm air heavily infused with magic slipped into the truck. Jacob walked to the gates and pressed his palms on the wood for only a moment before pushing them both open without effort.

I hadn't realized how ruined his clothes were. How much blood he had on him. He was physically fine—no wounds were bleeding and his heart beat steady, but he must have been exhausted, too. When he pushed the gates open, he turned to the car again, and I saw his face as if for the first time. Maybe it was just my weak eyesight, but he looked like a different person in daylight. So fucking young, I could hardly believe he was the same guy. Blond hair cut short, sparkling amber eyes, smooth shaved skin splattered with blood and grime...

Just whom had I trusted with my life here?

He got into the truck without a word and drove it right through the gates. A large yard was in front of me, at the end of which were two houses, one huge, the other tiny compared to it. They were both one story high, but the big one was so wide, I couldn't see the end of it. Three more trucks were parked in front of the houses. The grass was mowed, the trees in front of the wall that apparently went all around this property in perfect condition.

Jacob parked the truck next to the others and finally turned the ignition off.

He turned to me. "This is it."

"*What* is it?"

"Your new home," he said, and I could see him smiling through the corner of my eye.

Fisting my hands, I opened the passenger door. "Let's just get this over with."

I heard him chuckling as he got out of the truck. He thought this was funny. Great. I didn't even have the strength to pick him up and throw him all the way back to the gates again. See if he'd fucking chuckle then.

As it was, I had to wait for him to lead the way to the end of the wide house. There were no doors on the wall we could see, so I imagined this was the back. They did have windows, but thick black blinds were drawn behind all of them so I couldn't see anything. The only thing I could smell in this place was *magic*.

But the closer we got to the other side of the house, the better I heard. If it had been nighttime, I'd have heard all those heartbeats the second I got out of the truck. As it was, I was caught off guard by what I saw when we stepped behind the house.

And *who*.

Five other people were standing there, watching me. Well, not *people*, exactly. Not all of them, at least.

I stopped in my tracks, heart skipping a beat. I'd lost all of my knives and I had barely any energy left. The realization hit me like a slap to the face—I would never be able to fight them all and survive it.

Unless...

The first guy on my left, closest to the house, was skinny and tall, dark hair tied behind his head. He wore no shirt, just a pair of old sweatpants a size too big. Sweat covered his pale skin like he'd been running for hours. The guy next to him was bigger, bulkier, eyes so green they gleamed under the sunlight. He had all his clothes on—and a smirk on his face as he watched me.

Next to him was the third guy, just as big as his friend and even taller, hair cropped so short it looked like a shadow over his skull, his face crisscrossed with scar tissue everywhere. His hands were fisted tightly, and his eyes seemed to darken as they scrolled down the length of me.

The woman a few feet to his side was...*strange*, to say the least. Her hair was long and dark green, her eyes almost completely yellow, and her skin was pale and smooth for the most part. But there were greenish scales on the sides of her neck and the backs of her hands. She was tall and slim, leather boots up to her thighs, and tight clothes to reveal every curve of her body. In the dark, I was sure I'd be able to see exactly where else she had those scales on her skin. She was smiling sneakily as she looked at me from under her lashes, the wind blowing her green hair to the sides slowly like she was underwater.

But even she wasn't as strange as the last...erm, *wolf*. He stood on all fours atop a pile of rocks farthest away from the house, long grey fur covering every inch of him, wide brown eyes zeroed in on me. He didn't look like an ordinary wolf, either—he was much bigger, over four feet tall at the shoulders, his ears larger, his muzzle shorter, and his teeth way, *way* bigger than those of a normal wolf, coming out of his jaws and pointing in all directions. He growled low in his throat and lowered himself a bit, as if he were preparing for an attack.

I looked at them again, but I had nothing to say. I had nothing to even *think*.

"Who's that?" the woman asked, and when her lips moved, I saw her tongue—green, just like her hair, long and thin, like a fucking reptile.

"This is Nikki. She's joining the team," Jacob simply said, and he started to walk ahead.

I put my hand on his chest to stop him.

"What team?" This was *a team*? He hadn't mentioned a team before. I'd have remembered.

"This team," Jacob said, looking down at my hand on his chest, before he looked up at me, brows raised, a sneaky smile on his face. I fucking hated that stupid smile.

"She's a vampire," the bulky guy said, slowly crossing his arms in front of him, looking at Jacob now like he was demanding answers.

"She's been touched, too," Jacob told them.

Touched, *too*?

I looked at the others again. They were all touched? What in the hell?

"Still a vampire, Jay," the biggest of the bunch said with a growl, his scars making him look more intimidating than he actually was. My gods, he had so much hatred for me already. It made me sick and the whispers in my head grew a bit louder, but the moment he looked at me, I winked. If he wanted trouble, I was all up for it. Screw stopping myself —I couldn't if I tried in this condition. If they wanted to fucking die, they would.

"And part of this team," Jacob said, his voice lowering as he looked at the guy, like he was sending him some secret message.

"A fucking *mess* is what she is," the woman spit, looking down at my torn clothes in disgust. "Bloodsucker," she muttered under her breath.

I grinned. "Could be worse. I could look like you."

She hissed, letting out her tongue, and it was way longer than I imagined. At least a few inches when it left her mouth.

"Thanks. Now I'll never eat again," I said, so disgusted at the sight of that thing I was already nauseous.

"That's enough," Jacob said. "I'll talk to you in a bit. Come on, Nikki. Let's get inside."

But before either of us could take a single step, the wolf raised his head to the sky and howled. It was so sudden, I had to force myself to stand in one place and not jump back at the sound of it. It pierced right through my brain, and my mind was still echoing, even when he turned and jumped off the pile of rocks and started running to the other side.

The other side that I'd barely noticed until now.

The large area was divided into three parts. All of it for training, though much different from what we had at the Redwood castle. I couldn't see much because the sun was in my eyes, but I did see the wooden pillars, the chains all over the place, the white sand and the large rocks separating the three circles. Behind it were trees, trees, and more trees. The wolf went through them lightning fast and disappeared from my view completely.

When Jacob walked toward the house, I followed, eyes on the other four sorcerers still.

I walked backward through the wooden double doors just to make sure none of them would try to sneak up on me. In the condition I was in, I apparently couldn't trust my ears to warn me in time.

But nobody attacked me, and Jacob closed the door.

That didn't mean I felt safer—on the contrary.

"What the hell is this, Jacob? You never said anything about a team," I spit.

He sighed, holding his hips. "We didn't exactly have the time to talk details," he told me. "But yes—that is my team. They're all sorcerers who've been touched by Vein spirits, same as you."

I forced a smile. "And you're taking advantage of them same as you're doing with me?"

His brows narrowed. "I am not taking advantage of anyone. They all chose to be here. So did you."

Yeah—because he threatened to fucking kill me if I didn't do what he asked. And because he promised to give me what I wanted most if I did.

"What is this place?" I asked, despite my feelings. I was already in this mess. Hopefully by the end of the week, I'd be free for real and I could go back to my *real* home.

I could go back to Ax.

"It's where we keep ourselves hidden. Nobody around us can see or hear anything while the wards are up," he said and walked down the narrow corridor lined with doors.

Having no other choice, I followed. It smelled like

everything in here—sweat, dust, food, magic. Even dog hair, which I imagined came from the grey wolf.

Fuck, an actual wolf. An *animal*.

"This is you," Jacob said when we reached the door before last at the end of the hallway. "I'll show you the rest when you wake up."

"I am *not* sleeping in this place." Fuck that. I'd be stupid to trust any of them.

But Jacob turned to me. "It's safe. You're under my protection."

I laughed and it came out twisted. "I don't need your fucking protection." He'd been there. He saw me. The *other* part of me.

Which was…kind of the same as that wolf, actually. Not in shape, but a monster still.

"You do when the sun is shining and you're in a house full of sorcerers. *Touched* sorcerers," he said, but he wasn't amused. It was like he *forced* himself to say those words. To threaten me. Like he didn't really want to, but he knew he *had* to.

I doubted he could get any more annoying in the following days.

"I'll be fine. I don't need to sleep anyway." I did, but I could teach myself. Ax had done it. I could do it, too.

Jacob took in a deep breath. "I give you my word that nothing will happen to you while you're here. I swear it on my soul."

My gods, he was serious. He meant every word.

I squinted my eyes at him. "Hiding from what?"

He was surprised. "Excuse me?"

"You said that this was where you hid. What are you hiding from?"

He lowered his head. "There will be time for that. You

need to sleep, and so do I. When we wake up, we'll swear a formal blood oath. That will make the both of us feel better."

Right again.

And he turned to leave down the hallway.

"That wolf," I said before I could help myself. "That woman...they..." They were *like me*. Not exactly like me, but close.

I always thought that touched sorcerers would look possessed, like the humans do in movies. It was part of the reason why Jones's theory about me had always seemed impossible. Why I had been so quick to decide that Marie couldn't have been touched, either. She looked *normal*. Not possessed.

"That's Ray and Fallon," Jacob said. "Some Veins spirits never alter physical appearances, but some do. I think you're all pretty much the same."

I flinched. "Except I'm a vampire."

"Go to sleep, Nikki. Everything will be clear soon enough."

As much as I wanted to keep him there and ask him questions, just so it all felt a bit more real, or even made a bit more sense, I couldn't. I needed to lie down. I needed blood. I needed food.

I needed Ax.

Squeezing my eyes shut, I slammed the door of the room shut and let go of a long breath.

The room was small, those black blinds drawn all the way in front of the windows. The darkness felt mighty good, but the heat wasn't doing me any favors. Dust layered the dresser, the nightstand, and the windowsills around me. The white sheets on the tiny twin bed smelled, too, but I was in no condition to complain right now.

I was here. If I didn't let myself lie down and close my eyes, I would never make it out of here in one piece. I'd always been confident in my abilities to survive any given situation because of what I was, hence why Jones had even sent me here in the first place.

But now, things had changed. I apparently wasn't the only monster of my kind in the world.

And I apparently was really, truly *touched*.

Here I thought the day when I'd admit that to myself would *never* come, but it would be stupid to keep pretending at this point.

I lay down on the bed, eyes closed even before my head hit the pillow. I wouldn't be able to keep myself from sleeping, no matter how determined my own self—or the monster inside me—was.

But it was okay. I didn't trust Jacob, but I was making peace with the fact that I could die here today. And if that truly happened, at least I wouldn't have to feel anything.

CHAPTER
FOUR

I didn't die.

Couldn't figure out if I was relieved about it, or just disappointed. Too many emotions and I'd never been good at managing those. I literally didn't know what to think yet, but I was breathing. My heart was beating. The moon reigned over the sky now, and I'd cleaned myself up, too.

The bathroom was across the hallway from my room, as Jacob so kindly showed me when he came to my door just as night fell. And when I went back inside my room again, wrapped in towels, I saw he'd left gifts for me.

Clothes...and blood.

I rushed to it so fast, the glass almost slipped from my hand. The blood—cow blood—was cold and thick, but it was blood. And as much as my tongue hated the taste of it, my body came alive the second I took the first sip. Then I downed all of it in one swig.

Now, if I only had a bottle of vodka, too...

The clothes were a nightmare. Jeans that were made for men but small enough to fit me, and a large white shirt that fell all the way down to my thighs. But the worn sneakers fit, at least. It looked like I would have to go do some shopping here somewhere.

Except...shit. I didn't have my bag anymore. I didn't have any money.

Pulling the shirt up, I tied it right below my boobs just to give myself the impression that I was a woman. And even though it was nighttime, the air was too hot for my liking still. Must be all that magic hanging in the air, but I needed to loosen up. So, I tore the jeans around my thighs, too, and now they were practically shorts. Much better, though they were still pretty ugly.

When I felt ready enough, I stepped in front of the door and took in a deep breath.

This was it. I was in possibly the strangest place in the world, with people who were monsters, just like me. I no longer felt so special, and the more I thought about it, the more it seemed that I was actually *glad* about it. It wasn't just me. There were others out there. And if anyone in the world had actually been separated from their spirit, then there was a chance I could be, too.

That was the only motivation I would ever need, so I opened the door and stepped outside.

The house was empty, but I heard all six heartbeats right outside the doors. I walked slowly, unsure whether they could hear me, unsure what their spirits made them, how much it altered them. Unsure of *anything*, really. I took in the living room and the kitchen, the large fridge so full of delicious food, my mouth was watering. But not yet.

I didn't let myself hesitate. I opened the door and walked outside with my chin up, and they all stopped talking at the same time. All their eyes turned to me, and they all raised their brows at my outfit, like showing skin offended them. It made me smile. I was already feeling better.

"What happened to the wolf?" I asked, eyes on the only man I had never seen before—not in *this* shape. He had been a wolf earlier today, howling out his guts at the sky. But now he was a man. A drop-dead gorgeous man, too—with slightly long hair, black and the same kind of grey as his wolf's fur mixed together, big brown eyes that looked like melted chocolate. He wasn't as big as ScarFace there, but he was well built.

And he wasn't smiling at all.

"That's Ethan," Jacob told me, like he really thought I cared.

I smiled wider. "I preferred you as a wolf, Ethan." I really did. It made me feel less of monster, to be honest.

He showed me his teeth and snapped his jaw at me as if he didn't remember that he was only a man right now. It made me laugh.

Gods, it felt good to have blood in my veins and no sun to suck the energy out of me.

"Don't be rude, Nikki," Jacob said. "That's Dylan." He nodded at the tall skinny guy who'd been covered in sweat earlier. Now, he smelled clean, and he was actually wearing a black hoodie. Good for him. "Ray," he continued, looking at ScarFace. "Fallon, and that's Garret." The woman looked down at me just like before, and GreenEyes sneered at me. I winked at them.

"I honestly couldn't care less, but I'm sure it made you happy," I told Jacob. "The oath. I'm ready for it." And then we could get to work, because I was already impatient.

Jacob looked at me for a moment, as if he wasn't sure I was serious. When he saw that I was, he smiled, shaking his head. "Sure, Nikki. Let's do the oath. Follow me." And he started walking toward the three sand-covered arenas. I could see them in much more detail now that it was nighttime.

"You should have never come here. You're gonna die, you know that?" the guy Garret said to me as I passed him by.

Moving too fast for him to see, I stepped in front of him, way too close. I heard his heart tripping all over itself, smelled his fear just fine, even though he didn't move a single inch. I grinned, licking my lips.

"If I do, I'm taking all of you with me," I promised him in a whisper.

The others heard it, too—except Jacob, who was already five feet away. I thought one of them might attack me, and I was ready to show them exactly why they needed to stay the fuck away from me. Yeah, they were touched, but they were still sorcerers. They still moved slowly. They had bodies I could decapitate.

But even though I smelled the spicy scent of magic leaking from them, they didn't attack.

"Nikki," Jacob called, and I moved away from Garret, who was trying to rip me apart with his eyes. No longer afraid, but he was angry. So deliciously angry, I wanted to laugh in his face.

Fortunately for him, I had better things to do.

"Do you *have* to be so hostile?" Jacob said when I approached him, and he led us toward the round area in the middle, the ground covered in smooth white sand.

I laughed. "You think *that* was hostile?" I hadn't even drawn blood out of any of them. Hadn't even touched them.

"Like it or not, they're in this with you, okay? Just...try not to provoke them. Will you?" He stepped in front of me, brown eyes wide and honest. I rolled mine.

"Sure thing. Keep them off my back, and I won't talk to them—promise. But if *they* provoke *me,* I will kill them, Jacob. You can count on that." I really hoped he believed me, because I wasn't kidding.

With a sigh, he shook his head. "They're not that easy to kill."

I shrugged. "I'll try, anyway."

"Not everyone is your enemy. You know that?" he whispered.

"And if you're done lecturing me, we can get on with it."

He held my eyes for a moment, and my instincts were on high alert. Even the voices in my head didn't like the look on his face. There was just something *sneaky* about it, but he finally nodded.

"Step back. Let me mark the ground. Then we can start."

Three minutes later, he'd *drawn* some symbols on the sand between our feet, shapes I couldn't even make out properly. But when he rose again and took out a small army knife from his back pocket, I felt the magic coming off the sand in waves.

And I was already panicking.

Magic. It got shit done, yes, but it was also unpredictable. How did I know what went on in this guy's head? How did I know that he was really doing an *oath* and not something else entirely?

Get it together, I told myself in my head, pushing the voices down with all my strength. I was here. I'd agreed to this. I would see it through, no matter what.

When Jacob cut his thumb, he offered me the knife. The cut barely stung. I watched Jacob let a drop of his blood fall on the sand, right on the symbols he'd made, and the magic that connected with it hissed. I did the same, feeling the heat of it more by the second on my naked legs. When my blood reached the magic, too, it almost felt like it *exploded* into a large heat wave, coming up to my face, cutting off my breath. It took all I had not to back off.

"I, Jacob Mathias Thorne, give my word that I will protect you while you're in my house and will perform the ritual that will separate you from the spirit residing in your body, after you complete your end of this deal to help me fight against the biggest threat to the world of our time. May my word be my bond," he said and squeezed his thumb once more until another drop fell on the sand.

"That's it?"

He nodded. "That's it."

I sighed. "I, Nicole Arella, give my word that I will help you fight against the biggest threat to the world of our time, so that you will perform the ritual that will separate me from the spirit residing in my body," I said. "How's that?"

"Good. Now, *may my word be my bond,*" he said, and I repeated after him. Then I squeezed my thumb, the small cut already half closed, until another drop of my blood hit the sand.

The magic hissed. It suffocated the air for a moment, sticking uncomfortably to my throat, but it didn't last long. All in all, it was way easier than I'd thought it would be.

Jacob took the knife and put it back in his pocket. "All done," he said.

"What happens if I, say, *break* this oath?" Not that I was planning to, but I was curious.

Jacob looked at me pointedly. "You'll be drawn to me, and I'll be drawn to you until we've done what we swore to do. You can only escape a blood oath if I release you from it, or if you die."

"Good," I said with a nod because that went both ways.

I wasn't the only one that oath was tied to. "Now where's this *greater evil* that's got you so scared, sorcerer?"

His eyes gleamed as he smiled, but he didn't answer.

The symbols drawn in the white sand in a circle around me looked like child's play, even more senseless than the ones he'd made for the oath. Jacob kept moving his stick around the sand while I watched him, unsure whether to burst out laughing yet. Did he really think *that* was going to keep him safe from me?

"I still can't tell if you're serious," I told him, half my attention focused on the house, and the five sorcerers in front of it, watching us from the distance.

"Just bear with me. I know what I'm doing," Jacob said. But it *really* didn't look like it.

"What about if I do this?" And I ran my foot over the sand where he'd drawn a strange square symbol.

The symbol was instantly gone.

Jacob sighed. "Don't do that, Nikki." And he went back to drawing it again with his stick. "I haven't activated the magic yet. You won't be able to do that then."

His control of himself was really admirable.

"It's not going to work," I reminded him, just like I did when he told me his ridiculous plan—he wanted me to try to *control* the monster inside me, and that we wouldn't be able to go after anything or anyone until I did.

"It will. I know it will." Yep. His mind was made up.

"Jacob, much stronger people than you have tried." Master Ferrera—even Ivan. I'd killed three soldiers while they'd tried to contain me. Tried to *teach me* control.

Even they had given up after the second time.

"But have they tried with magic?" Jacob said, looking up at me.

"Brute strength." Which was better than magic...wasn't it?

The asshole grinned. "You care an awful lot about me and them." He nodded his head toward the house and the five sorcerers watching.

I rolled my eyes. "I really don't. But if I kill you, who's gonna get rid of this thing inside me?"

"Just trust me, okay?" he said and finally stood up, throwing the stick away and dusting off his hands. Torches were around us, and the fire burning in them cast shadows all over his face, making him look much older somehow than in daylight. Maybe it was a magic spell?

"I might have agreed to come here with you, but I'm not a damn fool." Of course, I wouldn't trust him.

"Then let me show you. Stand in the middle," he said, pointing at the circle I was in.

I did as he asked, only because I was really hoping to show him once and for all that this was stupid, couldn't be done, and we should get to the important stuff.

He raised his hands toward me and closed his eyes for a moment.

"I don't need to control anything," I tried again, for one last time. "Just take me to whatever needs killing and I'll take care of the rest." Or the monster that lived inside me would.

"It's not so simple," he told me.

"But it is. It's much simpler than this."

"You have no idea what you're talking about, Nikki. This isn't what you've seen or even what you can imagine."

"Then *tell* me what it is." What kind of monster had

scared him so shitless? Surely it wasn't worse than that wolf. Or that reptile woman.

Or *me*.

"Will you just let me do this?" Now he sounded irritated, too. Served me right for trying to *warn* him.

I sighed. "Fine. Go ahead. Knock yourself out." I'd warned him. My conscience would be clean when he died.

The air charged with a new wave of magic, this one even spicier. Jacob's eyes were closed, and for a second, I could have sworn the ground beneath my feet vibrated. The sand around me, especially around the symbols Jacob had made with his stick, began to shift slightly, too.

My mouth opened to tell him that. Surely it couldn't be anything good. But before I made a single sound, a yellow shimmer began to rise from the ground all around me, right over those stupid symbols.

Jacob had his eyes squeezed shut, sweat beads glistening on his forehead as he gritted his teeth, raising his outstretched hands higher every second. So much magic in the air, it was threatening to suffocate me. I brought my hand to my mouth, but it was no use. And the shimmer kept climbing higher, wrapping all around me like a fucking dome. Like that green bubble Jacob had created around us in North Dakota.

My instincts were screaming. The voices in my head were screaming, too. I gritted my teeth to try to keep control, and watched, half terrified, half mesmerized as the shimmer connected right over my head, encircling me completely. It was beautiful to look at, and maybe that's why I raised a hand to touch it.

It was hotter than real fire, and it burned my fingertips before I even made contact.

The voices in my head were going nuts.

"Jacob…" I warned, as the other five slowly approached us. Now I was stuck inside all that magic…*a goddamn mistake.*

What the hell was I even thinking, agreeing to this? They could do to me whatever they wanted right now, locked in all that magic. I was fucking *easy* to kill by any of them.

"Relax," Jacob said, breathing heavily now that he'd lowered his hands. "It's just a shield. It will keep both you and us safe."

"Yeah. A little mouse trap for the little mouse," the werewolf asshole said with a wide grin. He and the rest were right there behind Jacob now.

"You smell like wet dog hair, puppy," I told him. "And I really hope you enjoy the show."

It only made them all laugh, but it was okay.

"Silence," Jacob demanded, and they all clamped their mouths shut. The fear that joined the rising panic inside me had my entire body itching. The voices in my head were relentless, and for once, I didn't push them back. I didn't want to. If Jacob and his friends were hoping to kill me right now, I wanted to at least make it hard for them. And I couldn't do that by myself, not with all this magic around me.

I met his eyes. "See you in hell."

And I let it all go.

My fangs were already out, and the pain that started in my chest expanded all over me lightning fast. I welcomed it for once in my life, and it made it a bit easier.

"Nikki, wait!" Jacob said when he realized I was shifting, but it was already too late.

My legs shook before they let go of me. My knees sank in the sand as the monster took over, no longer held back by my mind. I let it all go, even as I hissed from the pain burning me like fire underneath my skin. And I felt my own body changing, too. Bones rearranging themselves, skin itching as it thickened, back hunching over.

To me, it all felt like it lasted an eternity, but it was over in about ten seconds.

And when it let go of me, I was breathing heavily, standing on all fours, watching them through the magic of the dome shimmering even brighter now that my eyesight was enhanced.

None of them were laughing anymore. Oh, no—they were *terrified* at the sight of me, and the monster in me liked it. I liked it, too. That's why we smiled at them and slowly stood up on two feet. I could hear their hearts beating in their chests. I could hear the blood rushing in their veins, the heavy magic that infused every cell in their bodies. I could almost hear the thoughts in their head, too, their instincts telling them to run, get away from me. Just move.

And...they did.

I stepped closer to the shimmery magic, looking from one to the other until I saw *all* of them in detail—even the scales underneath the tight clothes of the reptile girl. She had some on her shoulders, around her ribcage, and on her knees, too.

They moved back in unison, never even blinking their eyes, afraid they'd miss my movements. The monster in me relished the fear leaking from their pores. It *lived* for this. And I couldn't exactly say I wasn't enjoying the look on their faces, too.

"Nicole."

Jacob's voice took my attention, and I turned to look at him. Out of all of them, he was the only one who hadn't moved away. Maybe because he'd already fought me. Or maybe because he didn't have a spirit inside of him to warn him about me.

Because I remembered. In that dark alley with Ax, the spirit watching me, then crying out before it *ran* from me. I was willing to bet anything that *these* spirits trapped in those bodies were telling the sorcerers to do the same.

"Nicole, I know you're in there," Jacob said again.

I was no longer in full control of my body, so I was just as surprised as him when I saw my hand rising, pale skin covered in black veins, fingers tipped with black claws. And I ran those claws on the surface of the magic shield slowly.

Sparks flew. My smile widened. It was just magic. It wasn't unbreakable.

And when I broke this shield, they…

No.

That thought was all mine. *No, no, no*, I repeated to myself over and over again, but what good did it do when I wasn't the pilot of this body anymore? That's why I felt my hands fisting tightly before I slammed them both on the magic with all my strength.

My strength was *a lot* more now than usual because I wasn't just a vampire anymore.

"Stop it," Jacob said, reaching for the holster strapped to his back, under his jacket, and he pulled out two daggers —not the same ones he'd had with him that night we fought, but similar. Their blades were tipped, the metal engraved with symbols, similar to the ones he'd drawn on the sand around me. The magic in them hummed for a second as he activated it, and they began to glow orange. I remembered how much they'd hurt when they'd been inside me, but the monster didn't care. It wasn't afraid in the least.

"You will only hurt yourself," Jacob continued, but my

when they were sleeping, but it was so heavily guarded by magic, it just wasn't worth my efforts.

But at the side of it, there was a small opening in the rocks, almost like a hideout, and there was a small spring right in the middle of the stones that constantly fell on the moss and into the ground. It was so cold, nothing compared to it. That's why I always found myself there, splashing cold water on my face, on my neck, hoping it would clear my head.

It rarely did.

I sat on one of the larger blocks near it and just let the water flow down my fingers. It was somewhat calming, though it didn't get rid of the pain.

What was he doing? What was he thinking? Did he even wonder about where I was? Did he ever think about coming to find me? In the beginning, I'd expected him to storm through the gates every single hour. I don't know why, when I made him promise to take care of the siblings. Of course, he wouldn't be here looking for me. And it shouldn't have fucking *disappointed* me because he didn't owe me anything.

But what if he thought I'd forgotten about him? That I'd *left* him and ran away?

Did he wonder if he was ever going to see me again?

And...what if he'd moved on? Worse yet—what if he'd already mated with someone else?

Bile rose up my throat. I was going to throw up all that soup Jacob had made. Who put fucking broccoli in soup? Ugh, the taste of it was scandalous, but I ate it anyway. It was better than anything else he kept in his fridge when he ran out of groceries. Maybe that's where he'd gone off to. Apparently, there was a small town about forty minutes away from here, and he went there once a week to get supplies. He bought me clothes there, too—men's shirts and shorts. Ugly as fuck, but I didn't really care. I hadn't felt like myself in a long time, anyway. What did it matter what clothes I wore?

It wouldn't to Ax. He'd want them off me as soon as he saw me. I knew he would.

The familiar ache between my thighs intensified. Fuck, my body missed him, too. I craved his touch worse than the cold blood Jacob got when he went to town for supplies. Sometimes it was from goats. Sometimes from cows. Sometimes from an animal I'd never drunk before, but it kind of felt like it would belong to a rabbit or something. And I had to keep gulping it down every single night because of how much energy I wasted when I let the monster out.

Too much. Way too long. And every night was getting harder. How long until I lost my damn mind and killed everyone here just to go back to him? Even if he'd moved on, forgotten about me, was with someone else, I still yearned to see him. I just wanted to see his stupid perfect face.

Fuck, when was that day going to come?

When I heard the gates opening from the back of the house and the sound of the engine, I knew it was Jacob. Not only because he was the only one who ever drove out of here, but because I already recognized the smallest sounds his truck made. The smallest sounds *he* made. His scent, too. That's what a fucking month will do to you.

Three minutes later, he made it to the front of the house. I heard his footsteps until he was by the entrance doors. He stopped there and waited a heartbeat.

"Where are you?"

Shaking my head, I picked up a small rock and threw it

toward the house. He'd hear it. He'd know where it was coming from.

And he started walking again.

"Hey," he said when he showed his face.

"We need milk. And eggs. And fresh bread. And...everything else, really," I said because, apparently, he hadn't gone grocery shopping like I'd hoped. I usually smelled the different scents on his hands.

"Yeah, I know. I'll get to that first thing tomorrow." He stopped in front of me. The stone I sat on was high, so we were almost eye level. "I got something for you."

He reached for his pocket and took out a black velvet box no bigger than the palm of my hand.

I raised a brow. "Before you get down on your knee, it's a no. Sorry, but you're not my type."

He threw his head back laughing. It made me think of when Ax laughed that sinfully sexy sound. The way it vibrated on my skin—and I got goose bumps at the memory even now. That fucking bastard. I missed him so much it hurt.

"Damn. Here I was, planning a proposal with a band and everything," Jacob said, blood rushing to his cheeks as his shoulders still shook with laughter. "Look at this." He opened the box and showed me what was inside.

A silver chain with a silver pendant. The pendant was a misshapen circle with holes all over, a single symbol engraved on it—and *badly* at that, like it was made by a kid. It buzzed with magic, too.

"What's that?"

"It's a charm." Jacob took the chain out of the box. "I had a friend of mine make this for you."

I narrowed my brow. "I don't like jewelry." Especially the kind infused with magic.

"It's not just jewelry. Its magic was designed to take root in your mind, your conscience, and enforce it even when your spirit takes over you." My jaw almost touched the floor. "It can help you, at least in the beginning, until you learn how to control it by yourself."

I grabbed the pendant in my palm. The warmth of it wasn't comfortable, but it didn't burn my skin. "You can actually do that?"

Jacob grinned proudly. "It's magic. Not the kind I work with, but it still works. As long as you keep it on, you will be able to control your spirit, at least for a little bit. Just to get you going."

Holy shit, that was amazing!

In fact...*too* amazing. Way too good to be true.

My smile dropped as I analyzed the engraved symbol. It was shaped somewhat like an A with the ends of it curved up, and the line in the middle was vertical. It went from the top of the pendant all the way to the bottom.

"It's not gonna work," I said reluctantly.

"We'll still give it a try."

I looked up at him. "When are you going to understand that it won't *ever* work?"

"It will. You're stronger than you think."

He came to sit next to me on the rock. Having him so close to me made me uncomfortable, especially when I could hear the way his heartbeat sped up slightly every time he touched me. Sometimes I wondered if he had a thing for me. Sometimes I wished I'd never have to find out.

"I know you really want to believe that, but I'm really not," I promised him. "It's already been a month, Jacob. It's getting harder to convince myself not to kill all of you every minute. How much longer until I lose control?" I spoke slowly just to make sure he got every word. "I am *not* a sorcerer. I can hardly keep control of my own self, let alone the spirit." He flinched, but I didn't stop. "Just fucking take me to whatever it is you're hiding from me and let me do it. We're wasting time here."

"Learning control is *not* wasted time, Nikki," he insisted. "Imagine how much more power you'll have when you can actually guide your spirit, instead of the other way around."

"Except I don't want to guide shit. I just want it out of me. I am not that person you believe I am," I said through gritted teeth. We'd had this conversation before—three times. He wasn't going to fucking get through to me.

And, apparently, I wasn't going to get through to him, either.

"Sure you are. I've seen you fight your own self every day around here. Every time the others teased you. Remember in the beginning?"

Yeah, I remembered. It had taken all of two days to scare them enough that they stopped whispering things my way when I passed by, and I hadn't even had to try that hard, either.

"You didn't lash out at them. You wanted to, but you held yourself back. None of them did that in the beginning. There were always fights, and none of them thought they could have control over their spirits, either. Now, they do. For the most part."

I knew that, but it was different. My spirit wasn't as easy to handle. Even Ethan who turned into a giant wolf at will had trouble focusing sometimes—I'd overheard a conversation—and his spirit didn't want to be anywhere near mine.

"I will end up killing someone, just so you know." And I was fucking tired of warning him, too.

Jacob didn't say anything for a little while. I stared at the silver pendant in my hands, wondering if it really could do what he said it would. It was worth the risk, wasn't it? This guy wasn't going to let me out of here until I learned to control the monster. Worse yet—even if he did, I couldn't leave because I still needed him to set me free before I could leave here.

All this bullshit had an expiration date. I'd see it through no matter what because I *needed* to be free.

I needed to be free to go back to Ax.

So, I put the chain around my neck, and the magic of it vibrated when the pendant fell on my chest. It wasn't as uncomfortable as I'd feared, but every inch of me was perfectly aware of it, anyway.

"Where do you come from?" Jacob suddenly asked.

It caught me by surprise, but I didn't answer.

"What kind of monster would turn a six-year-old?"

"The kind that lives inside me," I said with a flinch. "I turned myself."

"How?"

I looked at him. He liked asking questions.

So did I.

"When are you going to tell me what we're up against? Why do you have all these people here in the first place?"

"To teach them how to fight Vein spirits, mostly," he said, which was more than he'd shared in the past when I'd asked him about it.

"What kind of a man would bring *me* to this place, when you could just take me to kill whatever needs killing and be done with it?" He must have known it was a risk to bring me here with all his people. With himself. Because despite what he thought, he didn't know me. I was a vampire. He had no reason to trust me at all.

He looked down at his lap instantly. "We'll get to that soon," he whispered. In other words, he *didn't* trust me, at least not as much as he wanted me to think.

But it was okay. I was looking forward to getting over this part of the night, anyway, so I could curl up in bed with a good book.

So, five minutes later, his shimmery magic was locked tightly around me, and I let go.

CHAPTER
SIX

It worked.

Only a little bit, but it worked. The stupid silver pendant and whatever magic was inside it worked. For a second there tonight, I'd thought about stopping my monster from raising its fists and slamming them against the shield, and...it had. It'd stopped. Only for like three seconds, but it fucking *worked*.

My insides had practically turned to jelly from the heat of all that *hope* that had suddenly come alive inside me.

When I woke up from unconsciousness, I had a big smile on my face because of it.

Until I saw the yellowed ceiling and realized I *wasn't* outside, or in the room I was using in Jacob's house.

And as soon as I sniffed the air, I sat up with a jolt.

It smelled of fire and leather and paper. So much paper. So much ink. So much *space*.

"What the..." I whispered when I took in the oval-shaped room. The ceiling was high, the walls covered in shelves with about a million books on them. There were even more books scattered all over the three desks. The thick carpet under my feet was made of a thousand colors. The fireplace had a low fire burning in it to my left, and...

Jacob sat behind the desk in the middle of the room, large, floor-to-ceiling windows at his back showing me the half-moon in the sky, and he was writing something down in a big book.

"There you are," he said, never looking up from the pages.

"What is this place?" I said, even before I realized that I *knew*. It was the house—the small one none of us were allowed to go in.

I stood up slowly and took in all the books on the shelves, most covers made out of leather, most of them without any titles on the spines.

"I call it the database," Jacob said, dropping his pen as he sat back on his chair, stretching his arms over his head for a second. The old lamps at the corners gave off more than enough light for him, and the darkness enabled me to see everything in detail, too. He had cigars on his desk, which made sense. He often smelled like them. Two silver flasks were there, too, probably full of whiskey. And he never got *me* any alcohol when he went shopping, no matter how many times I'd asked him. Asshole.

There was also an old map at the corner of his desk, and one location was circled in red three times—Tonto National Park in Arizona. Was *that* where we were going to fight whatever he was afraid of, when I learned to control my spirit?

Knowing he wouldn't tell me if I asked—or worse, kick me out of this house, I turned to the books again. I was too curious about them to leave right away.

"What are these books?" I ran my fingertips over the spines, afraid magic would leak out of them and burn my fingers for a moment. Nothing happened. The leather of them was cold instead.

"Recordings of magic," Jacob said. "Of spirits, mostly. It was started by my ancestors over three hundred years ago. Passed down from father to son, mother to daughter."

I picked one of the books from the shelf, and he didn't stop me. No magic attacked me, either. So, I opened it.

"My family has always hunted evil magic users and Vein spirits. We've been recording every kind we've ever come across since this began. Right now, I'm filling up your file, too," Jacob continued.

I looked at the pages filled with black ink, but the words were all foreign to me.

"I can't understand shit," I said, closing the book again.

Jacob laughed. "They're in old Gaelic."

I raised a brow. "You're Irish?"

"Kind of," he said. I put the book back in place and went closer to his desk. Not only was he writing in that same language in black ink, but he had a drawing of me in my monster form, too. All hunched over, big black eyes, almost completely black skin. He'd put in so much detail—even the small veins on the sides of my neck.

I looked away from it immediately. I didn't want to see it.

"Ever heard of computers?" I asked instead.

"Ever heard of the Internet and how everyone can get their hands on anything digital if they really want to?" he asked instead. "Information like this could literally ruin the world if it fell in the wrong hands."

"I'm sure that's exaggerating it."

"Not really. Do you have any idea how many sorcerers out there think it's smart to summon Vein spirits?"

I laughed. "You're joking."

"I'm really not. Even humans who think they're summoning *the devil* draw out spirits all the time. There's all kinds of people out there," Jacob said, smiling as he shook his head. "Some think that spirits can prolong their lives or the lives of their loved ones. Some think they can use them to get rich. To gain more power. To have someone killed—you name it. They've done it at least once."

"Holy shit." Even *I* knew not to mess with Vein spirits, and I was a vampire. Technically speaking.

"Yep," he said. "But people are learning. Most of them, anyway." With a sigh, he picked up the pen again. "That shelf over there has some books in English. You can read them if you want."

"Really?" What happened to *you're not allowed through those doors*?

"I know how much you like to read. You're running out of books. I don't keep that much fiction in the house."

"And the ones you do keep are not the best, I'm afraid. You could use some help in the bookstore."

He snorted. "I've got enough to read here. I don't need more books."

I gave him a pointed look. "You always need more books."

"I thought you said you wanted to read."

And he was absolutely right. I went to the shelf in the other side of the room and picked up one of the thickest books on it. English.

I was so excited, you'd think he'd handed me human blood. With my face buried in the book, I went and sat on the same old couch I woke up on.

"I don't get why they don't teach us this stuff." If there were that many kinds of Vein spirits out there, vampires should be taught that, right? *Know thy enemy*, and all that.

"The same reason sorcerers don't teach their young about vampires anymore. They think we're separated forever."

I looked up at him for a second. "And we're not?"

Jacob thought about it for a second. He dropped his pen and picked up a cigar from his desk, and just spun it around with his fingers, looking intently at it. "All I know is, when dealing with preternatural things, one can never keep things under control for long."

"I suppose not. We're vampires. We're predictable. You know what to expect from us. You guys, on the other hand..."

"Magic can be predictable, too. At least that of most sorcerers," Jacob said. "You can know what to expect from it from the color alone most times."

That certainly got my attention. "I thought that was individual for every sorcerer."

"Not really. Certain spells have certain colors, and it's also an indicator of strength. White, for example, comes only with the highest level of power. Red, too. Paler colors, yellows and greens, serve to protect more than to attack. A spell to put someone to sleep would be a shade of purple. It still depends on the magic and the caster, but for most, that's how it is."

My, my. He was feeling very chatty tonight. Was it because he saw that I could actually control the monster a tiny bit earlier?

"What about *you*? You have colorful magic and also other things. You sometimes whisper words out loud, sometimes don't."

"There are spells that gain more power when you speak the words out loud. It takes a lot of you, but the magic comes out stronger," he said without hesitation.

"And your glowing daggers?" I continued.

"Family heirloom," he said. "The spell was designed by my great-great aunt." I'd thought it was a spell—the blades were engraved, and that's where the magic came from. My monster felt it perfectly.

"And whatever shield you had on that night, too. It was invisible, but my claws couldn't get through to you." Ax hadn't been able to get through to him. And my monster had tried to rip his face off, too. It hadn't worked.

Jacob grinned sneakily. "You're awfully curious."

I shrugged. "Aren't you?" He knew what I meant—if he could answer me, I could answer him, too.

"That's a blood spell I had put on me by my father the day I was born. Had to cut me open to be able to spell me properly, but his magic is inside me now. Same as his father's was in his body."

"And you're gonna pass it on to your son, too?"

"I hope so, if I ever become a father," he said.

"Why doesn't everybody else do the same spell?" No other sorcerer I'd met had been able to keep me away from them like that.

"The spell runs in the family. It was created by our blood and it only works on our blood. Like I said, my ancestors were all hunters. Every spell and every weapon they created was geared toward hunting spirits," he said. "This specifically is the most powerful shield out there that I've heard of. Nobody can break it when I activate it."

"Except it cracked," I reminded him. "My spirit heard it. The magic cracked while we were fighting." Which meant if I'd kept going for long enough, it would have given eventually.

Jacob nodded. "Which is why you're here."

Oh. "I see." That's why he'd changed his mind about

me. "And what about Marie?" I wondered. At that point, there was no doubt in my mind that she was really touched, but her transformation had been so...*specific*. "I saw her fangs. She moves as fast as vampires. She jumps high, too."

"I'm not sure, but there are all kinds of spirits in the Veins. I'd imagine there are plenty who are similar to vampires," he said, scratching his cheek. "If I had to guess, it was the same kind of spirit as Ethan's—and yours."

I shook my head. "Except I can't control mine. And Ethan always has trouble with his wolf, right?"

"Yes, but that doesn't mean it's not the same kind. That only indicates the level of power—the more powerful the spirit, the harder it will be to tame it, so to speak. Fallon, for example, has never had much trouble controlling hers—it always behaved according to her will."

I nodded as if I understood, but I didn't. Not yet, anyway.

"My turn," Jacob said in a rush before I could think of something else to ask him. "What's it like in the Hidden Realm?"

"Not much different from cities here. We have everything you have. Lots of livestock. Lots of vampires. Lots of booze."

"And the gates? How secure are they?"

I grinned. "Are you planning on marching into the Hidden Realm sometime, Jacob?"

I felt the chills rushing down his back. "Just wondering how safe it really is."

"It's pretty safe. Our rulers are strict. They don't kid around. There are those who manage to break through the magic and get away, but they always get caught. I'm pretty sure you know that."

He thought about it for a second. "Your rulers are strict, huh?"

"Very." I waited a heartbeat, curious to see where else he would take this. How much more he wanted to know. Maybe even figure out *why*. The Hidden Realm was none of his business. It was a world separate from this.

Why the questions?

But Jacob didn't ask me more about it. He wanted to, I could tell, but one look at my smile, and he held himself.

"I saw the spirit hesitate tonight," he said instead. "Was that you?"

"I think so," I said, afraid I'd jinx it if I talked about it. "I mean, it barely lasted three seconds, but I held it back."

"You've never been able to do that before," he whispered.

I tried not to smile as I nodded. "Never."

"Then the spell is doing its job. It will only get stronger the more you wear it."

Damn. I got the chills. *Even stronger*?

"Now, I need to get back to work," he said, dropping the cigar and picking up the pen again.

As much as I wanted to pick his brain, I also didn't want him to know exactly how hopeful that thing made me, or that I actually believed that it was doing something to help.

And I wanted to read that book on my lap, too. So, I stopping thinking about the pendant completely for now and turned to the pages.

Time must have passed faster than I realized because the next time I looked up, the sky had just started to turn grey, and I'd read almost half the entire notes in that book.

All those different kinds of Vein spirits—and they were all named according to the person they'd latched onto, everything Jacob's family had come across from 1920 all the way to 1932. So fucking fascinating, I could read *everything* in this room without ever getting bored. Almost better than fiction—except there was no description of hot guys or sex scenes in these pages. A shame, really.

To my surprise, Jacob was still awake, too.

In fact, he was sitting back in his chair, chewing on the bottom of his pen, watching me.

Just how long had he been staring at me like that?

I straightened my shoulders immediately, feeling a bit flushed. "Do you name all the spirits after the people they touched?"

"Yep."

"Is *my* spirit called by my name?"

He smiled. "Yep."

Well, that sucked. *The Nicole Spirit*. Didn't have a nice ring to it at all.

"Who is he to you?" Jacob asked, looking at me intently from under his lashes.

I shook my head, confused. "Who?"

"Savage Ax."

My heart tripped all over itself. Even more blood rushed to my cheeks instantly. The image of his face was right there in front of my eyes, as if summoned by magic. The blue of his eyes touched my soul, and it took a couple of blinks to be able to *unsee* him. Fuck, I missed him so much that just hearing his name being spoken felt like a knife straight to my gut.

"Why do you care?" I asked, suddenly aware that I'd spent literally all night locked up in a room with him. I moved too fast for him to even notice me before I put that book on his desk.

I held his eyes for a moment, and he held mine.

He looked tired. Exhausted. The bags under his eyes had turned into a deep blue.

But Jacob didn't answer.

I left the house feeling very strange—and not in a good way.

Why in the world would Jacob ask me about Ax after one month of living under the same roof?

I HEARD THE WHISPERS, but they were too far away still.

The moment my eyes opened with the new night, I heard them. They were coming from the other side of the house, but it was so silent everywhere else that the voices reached all the way to me.

I sat up, my body already on high alert. The silver pendant on my chest felt heavy, warm, foreign, but I still didn't take it off. I tiptoed to the door instead and pressed my ear to the wood to hear better, my breath held.

"*Slaughtered completely,*" someone was saying. I think it was Ray.

"*Not just that, but the fire, too,*" said Fallon.

"*You sure this is smart?*" That had to be Dylan, who rarely even looked at me. I liked him best.

"*It's already gotten out of hand.*" Ray again. "*But he's right. Night has fallen.*"

And they all scattered around the house the next second.

Night has fallen. Which meant whatever they were talking about, they didn't want *me* to hear it.

It wasn't that much of a surprise, to be honest. I hated their guts, they hated mine. I kept secrets from them, too.

But my instincts were screaming, and the voices in my head...

Well, shit, they were only whispering still.

I'd been living with them my whole life, which was how I knew that they should have been shouting by now. Why weren't they?

My hand rose, and I touched the silver pendant on my chest. Was it possible that that thing was giving me more control even when I was in charge of my body? *It will only get stronger,* Jacob said. Was he actually telling the truth?

Despite everything, my face broke into a smile. It was getting really hard to *not* believe that I could have a chance at controlling the spirit inside me. With this thing on, I actually could.

As I went through the motions, I replayed what I'd read about spirits in that house. So many different kinds of them were out there, and with every new page I'd read, I'd felt less of a monster. Less *alone*. And just the thought that Jones knew about all of it and never told me, making me feel like I was the only freak of my kind out there in the world, made me cringe. I wondered what he'd say when I confronted him about it—because I would. He owed me some goddamn answers.

Would he even bother?

I remembered the conversation I'd had with Jacob, too. About his family, and magic...how he'd asked me about Ax.

Why? It hadn't sat well with me then, and it felt even weirder now. Why so curious after a whole month?

But the night wasn't done surprising me yet.

I found Jacob and the others in the kitchen when I left my room. As much as I wanted to ask him why he'd mentioned Ax, I bit my tongue. It would only give him the opportunity to ask again.

My nights here had become a routine, so my legs took me outside to the training area without my even having to think about it. I never ate with the others. I'd rather blow off some steam before dinner, anyway.

But Jacob followed me.

"We're leaving for a little while," he said, catching me by surprise. Hadn't he been out the day before?

"Oh, yeah?" I said as I turned to him. "Wait—who's *we*?" In the month I'd been here, I'd never seen any of them leave this territory. Unless they'd done it in daylight, but even then, I'd have been able to smell something different about them. They always smelled the same.

"Me, Ray and Fallon," Jacob said, and the way his heart was racing and the way his palms were sweaty, it was obvious that he was nervous about it, too.

I narrowed my brows, moving closer. "Why? You usually go out there alone."

"I know, but I'm taking them with this time. We'll train once we get back," he said, already walking backward. "Don't try anything on your own, okay?"

"Hey, wait a second," I said, a dumbfounded smile on my face. "What are you going to do? Why Ray and Fallon? Is something wrong?" Just...*why*?

"I have a Vein spirit close by that needs locking up. I'm simply taking them to make sure nothing goes wrong," Jacob said.

And...it was a *lie*.

I heard his heart. I heard his blood. I smelled his sweat perfectly.

The asshole was lying through his teeth.

He turned around, close to the corner of the house now, and before he could disappear from my sight, I moved at my full speed and materialized in front of him before he could take another step.

It *scared* him, too.

I grinned. "You're awfully easy to spook tonight." He usually wasn't.

"I'm in a hurry." He tried to get past me, but I moved in front of him again.

"You're lying to me, Jacob. You know I can tell, right?" He knew very well what I was. And the way his heart kept accelerating proved me right with every beat. "What's going on?"

"A spirit," he said, composing himself. "Not what you're here for."

"I don't care. Take me with. You know I can help."

But he shook his head even before I finished speaking. "No. You stay here."

"I'm a better fighter than Ray and Fallon," I reminded him.

He looked at me for a moment, then leaned in closer, whispering: "Stay here. I'll be back in no time."

When he walked around me again, I didn't stop him. I already knew him well enough by now—he wasn't going to budge.

Stay here, he said, like I was a fucking dog he could order around.

The door of the house opened, and the others came out, their eyes locked on me. My skin crawled as if I had a million spiders all over me. Fallon and Ray took after Jacob without a word, while Dylan, Ethan and Garret stood there in front of the door, arms crossed as they looked down at me.

My instincts were on high alert, so I moved without even realizing it. A seconds later, I stopped in front of them, and Dylan and Garret moved back, while Ethan, the mighty werewolf, held himself in place, gritting his teeth. The smell of his fear still reached me, though, but I didn't give a shit.

"Where are they going?"

"Out," Ethan spit.

"Out where?"

He forced a grin on his beautiful face. "Just out."

I smiled, too. "What were you whispering about tonight in the house?"

I could have slapped them, and they'd have been less surprised. Dylan lowered his head. Garret looked away, but Ethan still held my eyes.

"I won't hurt you, sweetie. Promise. You can tell me about it."

Out of all of them, Ethan was the easiest to get to. He had the most trouble containing his wolf spirit, and it kept him frustrated all day.

That's why I expected him to take the bait. I expected him to say something else, slip, give me a clue—*anything*.

But instead, Garret slapped the back of his hand to Ethan's arm, and the three of them walked inside the house, slamming the door shut in my face.

Jacob was already in his truck, the ignition on.

It was a second's decision.

He was hiding something from me, while I'd done nothing but try my damn best every single night here with him. I'd done everything he asked, had locked myself up in here for a whole month, because that was the deal. He wanted me to *trust* him, then he turned and lied to my fucking face.

My mind was already made up when I jumped and landed on the rooftop of the house. The dark of the night shielded me, and I made it to the other side in no time. The gates were open—Ray still standing by them to wait for the red truck to drive out, so he could close them again.

And that was my only shot. The wards would be up and running the moment Jacob drove away from this place. Would I be able to get through them on my own?

Better not find out.

As if possessed by a brand-new monster, I moved to the other side of the house and jumped to the ground, then climbed the eight-foot-tall wall that surrounded the property. The scent of magic still hung in the air, but the ward was inactive for now, and it didn't stop me when I reached the top.

The gates closed. Jacob drove his truck ahead. Magic sizzled in the air—the wards activating again.

I jumped.

CHAPTER
SEVEN

Ax Creed

I was nineteen when I walked inside a cage for the first time. The man I was in there with hadn't lost a single fight in his last nineteen matches. I found that funny, especially since he was twenty-four and over six foot three, one of his arms the size of both mine.

But Giuseppe de la Silva had no more money to waste feeding and clothing me. So, he decided now was the time for me to choose my fate—die right here in the cage or earn my right to live as his slave.

The crowd had gone nuts. All the bets were placed—all of them in my opponent's favor. Giuseppe wasn't even there to watch—*that's* how little faith he had in me. He knew I was going to die. Chances were he'd betted against me, too, though I never knew for sure.

And that did something to me.

He'd used me since I was nine years old—I'd cleaned, I'd cooked, I'd run errands, transported drugs and weapons for him, had been in jail for him three times, had followed behind him like a fucking puppy, had done everything he ever ordered me to do, but he always wanted more. Never satisfied, always hungry.

And now, after a decade, I was locked three stories underground in a cage in the middle of London with a monster who looked at me like he couldn't wait to eat me raw.

I thought it would scare me. I thought I'd be paralyzed by the fear alone and wouldn't even remember how to fight.

Instead, the look in the man's eyes fueled me. It took away everything I was, everything I knew, and something in my head switched.

In the moments before the fight began, I had a choice to make.

And I made it.

Fuck Giuseppe de la Silva. Fuck this guy who was looking at me like I was his favorite fucking meal. Fuck every bastard here who was screaming their guts out, cheering for him, and booing me.

I'd make them all regret having bet against me.

They all took what they wanted from me, and I'd had enough.

From that moment on, I decided I was going to take what I wanted, too.

And I really wanted this guy's left eye. It was bigger than the right, though it twitched every few seconds. It would serve me as a reminder that you could see the world in a million different ways. It was all about perspective. The power was in my mind. If I saw him as a dead guy, that's what he would be. If I saw myself walking out of here alive, I would be. It didn't matter what it took—I'd do it.

It was in those moments that I learned to set all of my limits on fire until they all burned to a crisp. *Whatever it takes.*

And seven minutes later, they opened the cage door for me. My opponent was dead, his left eye in the palm of my hand. I had broken ribs, a cracked jaw, several broken teeth, but I was standing. I had won.

I would *never* lose again.

The next day, Giuseppe's men told him that I'd fought like a *savage*. He'd thought that was the name that suited me best.

The next time I was in the cage, I was introduced as Savage Ax. They all bet in my favor. They all cheered for me. They all made money off me.

And I walked out of the cage alive a second time.

I walked out of the cage alive seventy-two times in total before Robert found me. I was merely human then.

Now, I wasn't, but my mind hadn't changed. It never would. I still didn't lose. *Whatever it takes.*

If that makes me a bad man, so be it. I'd rather be bad than be a fucking victim.

That's why I didn't mind watching the dead sorcerers in front of me as I sat in the recliner in their living room and sipped their whiskey. The three men had been hard to put down, I'll admit. I'd lost a lot of blood and there was still a little of their magic in my system. Nothing some warm human blood wouldn't take care of. All that mattered was that I'd walk out of this house alive.

I'd do whatever it took to find her.

"You could have just told me," I whispered, then laughed at myself. Dead men don't speak. It made me wonder if they even knew where Damsel was. If they'd just stopped to talk to me when I first came to their house tonight. If they'd just told me what I wanted to know instead of attacking me.

They'd chosen their fate, the same way I did mine.

And now, I'd set their house on fire and move on to the next sorcerers. One of them was going to tell me where Damsel was eventually.

One of them would...

Except it had been a month. I'd killed...how many sorcerers? I lost count after the tenth because does it really matter? I was going to kill all of them until I found her. I wasn't going to leave anything behind.

But in the past week, something kept nagging at my brain.

What if that sorceress locked under the Sangria castle in the Hidden Realm had lied through her teeth? What if she'd figured the best way to get rid of me was to get me out here, away from Marie and her brother? What if she hadn't felt shit—not my soul, not Damsel's heartbeat? What if I was out here chasing fucking ghosts?

I took the phone out of my pocket and checked the last message from Raphael. *Safe and sound*, it said. I'd put him and his twin brother Lucien in charge of the siblings. They had the wooden charms the sorceress had made to protect them, but one could never be too sure.

But as long as they were safe, living in my house, I'd be free to continue my search out here.

With a sigh, I stood up and grabbed the bottle of whiskey. Another dead end. How many more of them would they make me kill? I was getting tired. Worse—I was getting impatient. And bad things happened when I got impatient. Well...*worse* things.

Drenching the carpet with whiskey, I took the small box of matches from my back pocket. Last stick. I kept meaning to get a lighter, but there was just something about lighting up a stick, throwing it to the floor, watching the tiny flames expand and eat up an entire fucking house—with the sorcerers inside, just like they'd done with Damsel.

The fire spread on the carpet lightning fast. It would spread onto the bodies, too, and the recliner, which was right next to the curtains. Throwing the empty bottle of whiskey to the floor, I made to leave the house.

And I heard the first heartbeat right outside.

Stopping in my tracks, I closed my eyes and held my breath, focusing only on my ears. Two heartbeats. The scent of their magic barely reached me because of the fire burning behind me. More sorcerers. My lips stretched into a smile when I opened my eyes, staring at the closed door at the end of the wide hallway. It must have been my lucky fucking night.

But...

I heard the footsteps even among the crackling of the fire. I smelled the magic, raw and powerful—a kind I'd only ever smelled once before. An invisible fist hit me right in the gut, knocking the breath out of me as I waited. It felt like my whole life hung on the moment that door would open.

And...it did.

The door pushed aside with a weak cry, and in front of me was a man I'd dreamed about so many times one would think I was in fucking love with him.

Jacob Thorne, with his cowboy hat and his glowing daggers, stood barely ten feet away from me.

Laughter burst out of me as I threw my head back. I thanked the heavens and the hells and everything out there that cared. All my doubts and second thoughts vanished into thin air. The sorceress hadn't lied. If Jacob Thorne was alive, so was Damsel. They'd both been buried under that fire that night.

Damsel was *really* alive.

"You've really outdone yourself, Savage Ax," Jacob said as I laughed still. I couldn't imagine a time when I was happier. All I'd carried on my shoulders since that night he ambushed us turned light as a feather. It was only a matter of days now before I saw her. "I'll admit, I didn't think you had it in you."

My shoulders still shook with laughter, but the guy wasn't amused. His eyes moved back to the fire burning in the living room behind me, consuming everything in its path. The heat of it made the back of my leather jacket soft. It was close, but I didn't give a shit.

He was here.

I sat on the floor, shaking my head. Here I was, second-guessing everything, and he shows up and makes everything better. Out of all the people in the world, I never thought I'd be so damn happy to see his face.

"You know, you had me going there for a bit. You really did," I told him. "How'd you do it?" How had he kept Damsel's heartbeat from reaching me? I was actually really curious.

But Jacob flinched as he stepped into the house, slowly. "Isn't it enough to kill them?" He brought his hand to his nose as if to stop the smell.

I shrugged. "That's what you did with her, didn't you? Put a fucking house on her head then set it on fire. It's only fair."

"They put a house on *my* head, too. You don't see me going around killing them, do you?" he said. "It was just a few scared sorcerers—not *all* of them."

"Well, somebody has to pay for taking her from me." To me, they were all equally responsible.

"You're slaughtering people," he spit.

"And you knew what was going on all along. Could have come to stop me at any time, but you stayed away," I said with a grin. "So, don't fucking lecture me, cowboy. Just tell me where she is."

"She's dead," he said without hesitation, but his heart gave him away.

My smile widened. "Liar."

"This ends here, Savage," he said, slowly raising his daggers. Those hurt like a bitch, but last time, I hadn't really had the right perspective when fighting him. Now, I did. He didn't scare me. On the contrary—he just might be the guy whom I'd have the patience of the world to leave on that triangle stone back home to be cut in half.

"It really does—*if* you tell me where she is. I won't have to kill anyone else." It was the truth, and he could hear it.

He still didn't like it.

"Where she is, is in a *safe* place, far away from monsters like you," he said. My smile dropped instantly. "She's making her own new home, Savage."

I stood up again slowly. He was a fucking liar.

"Why do you think she hasn't come back yet, huh? You know her. Nobody would have been able to stop her if she wanted to come back to you. What does it tell you that she didn't?" He took another step forward. I was already seeing red. "Do you really think that anyone in the world would be able to love someone like you? Someone who does *this* to innocent people?"

Something snapped inside me, and it echoed in my mind. Something that insisted that *he was right*.

Damsel was not the kind of woman you stopped. If she

wanted something, she was going to go against the whole fucking world to get it. Nobody stopped her.

Not even Jacob Thorne.

Unless…she really didn't want to come back to me.

"That's right," Jacob said, coming closer. "She's choosing to stay with me, Savage. It's her choice. All these people you've killed are gone for nothing. Now, *you* will go for nothing, too."

I felt the magic a second before the red smoke made its way toward me lightning fast. Whether I could move away or not didn't matter—I *didn't* want to. The magic slammed onto my chest, knocking me on my back, the flames burning the carpet barely inches away from the top of my head.

She didn't want to come back to me.

"You should have stopped when you had the chance."

My instincts took over. I didn't even have to think about it before I found myself on my feet, fangs extended, vision zeroed in on Jacob, and the glowing dagger coming for my chest. I moved as if in a dream. I stepped aside and hit the hallway wall with my shoulder, then ducked when he swung his other dagger for me.

I moved away, limbs heavier with all the magic emanating from his body, but still way too fast for him to catch me when he swung his daggers. I didn't hit him. Didn't try to stop him. My body was on autopilot, and it was almost fascinating to see how well I fought even without thinking. It was in my blood. I'd been doing it since I was ten years old, and my body couldn't forget even if my mind was wiped clean.

Thoughts spun in my head. I breathed and my heart beat, but it occurred to me every new time Jacob came for me that I was already a dead man if I believed that Damsel had chosen to stay away from me.

But I didn't *really* believe it, did I?

When he swung both daggers at my face, I ducked, then grabbed his arms as I came up. "Tell me where she is," I demanded.

If I could see her, if I could talk to her, if she could tell me herself, I wouldn't have to wonder. I'd know for sure.

But Jacob slammed his forehead onto my nose instead. I stepped back, stars in my vision only for a second. A second was all he needed to summon his magic again and hit me square in the face—this time twice as hard because we were closer. That's why I flew in the air, through the fire, and slammed onto the wall on the other side.

My clothes were melting. My hair smelled, too. I pushed myself up looking at the fire around me. Hell, as hell should be, except to me, it was nothing compared to the hell inside my head.

She would tell me. If I saw her, I would see it in her eyes. I would smell it on her body. I would hear it in her heartbeat.

Whether Jacob was lying didn't matter. I had to see for myself. I had to make sure she was safe.

And if he thought this fire was going to stop me from finding her, he really had no fucking idea about who I was.

I didn't really see anything, and the crackling of the fire trying to melt my skin off made it impossible to hear his heartbeat, but I jumped anyway. Jaws open, fangs ready, I jumped as far as my body allowed. And the moment I rose a couple feet in the air, I saw him and his glowing dagger, looking at the fire in the living room, trying not to breathe in the smoke.

He only saw me a split second before I slammed onto him with all my strength.

We rolled on the ground down the hallway, arms locked around each other. But I knew if I stayed that close to him for long, he was going to gather his shit and start swinging those daggers at me. I tried to bite him on the shoulder, but whatever magic protected him didn't let my fangs sink in his skin, only his clothes.

So, I had no choice but to let go of him and push him farther away while I jumped to my feet. The living room was a blazing inferno now. If either of us was going to survive, we needed to take this outside. The smoke made it impossible to breathe properly.

Jacob rolled a couple more times before he made it to his feet, right in front of the open door. We were barely three feet away from one another and the fire was coming.

I smiled. "Brought your minions again, I see." There were two hearts beating right outside, hiding from my view.

And Jacob stepped back. "I did, as a matter of fact," he said, walking backward onto the driveway, his eyes never leaving mine as I came out of the house, too.

Finally, fresh air. Cold air.

And two people at the end of the driveway.

I raised my brows at the sight of the woman, the unusual green of her hair, the scales on her hands and neck. The guy by her side was bigger than me, bulkier, much like the guy I'd killed in my first cage fight. I wanted this one's left eye, too.

"Last chance, Jacob," I said as his minions came closer. "Tell me where she is, and I'll leave you alone."

But Jacob didn't tell me shit. Instead, he put his daggers in his holster, and raised his hands toward me.

His minions did the same.

I smiled, raising my arms. Which way was the magic going to come from first? How much would it hurt?

It didn't really matter. I'd take it.

And then I'd pick them apart one by one.

CHAPTER
EIGHT

NIKKI ARELLA

HAVING to run for three fucking hours all the way to Iowa wasn't fun. Cars weren't that fast compared to a vampire, but it still sucked ass to have to run behind it, keeping just the right distance so Jacob wouldn't know I was following. It had been stupid of me, knowing what happened the last time I was out here, but I'd jumped.

Then, I'd have no choice but to keep on going, wondering why in the world it took so little for me to convince myself to do the *wrong* thing. Never the right thing, no—just the wrong.

It had to be that house. I'd spent an entire month locked up in that place, and it had gotten to me. All of it had just gotten to me, even more so than I'd realized. Because right now, I was out here, with no walls surrounding me, and I *never* wanted to go back.

Would it really be smart of me to run away now, after everything?

I didn't even get it. I'd been locked in the Hidden Realm my whole life. It was an entire city, but even so, I should have been able to stay in Jacob's house without feeling like I might spontaneously combust any second.

It's fine, I told myself. It's okay. I knew the way—I could go back to Minnesota before Jacob got there. And I could jump over the wall when he disarmed the wards to get the car through the gates, too, same as I'd come out. He would never even know I left.

And the way I sounded just now to my own self made me think I was *afraid* of Jacob.

Fuck that—I wasn't. And if he found out...well. He'd think twice before lying to me again.

I walked ahead with my head high, enjoying the silence of the night. It was almost midnight, and we were in a small town at the edge of Iowa. I'd dodged this one on my way to Atlanta with Ax, but it was nice. Quiet. Small houses, the people inside sleeping. I heard their heartbeats, but I didn't even get the urge to take their blood. Jacob kept me well fed, at least. And now that I hadn't had a sip of alcohol in a month, I was starting to see how much power I'd willingly given it by thinking I *couldn't* function without it.

Sometimes, my own self surprised me.

Maybe that pendant had something to do with it, too. I touched it from over my shirt, as if to make sure it was there, even though I felt it against my skin. Still as warm. Still as much magic leaking from it. I didn't even hate it anymore. In fact, I was starting to think it was the best thing I was ever given.

In the distance, something moved.

I stopped and looked up, sure that it had been a bird or something, but when I saw the smoke rising in the sky, my heart caught in my throat. It was just a little bit, the tendrils spiraling up to the sky, but it meant there was a fire under it.

I strained my ears to hear a car noise. Jacob had stopped his truck—I'd heard it. It's why I'd slowed down, too. And I could see his damn red truck parked just at the end of the narrow street.

But then I heard the voices. They were barely there, and I couldn't understand anything they were saying, but the night was so quiet that it was impossible to miss the sound. I took off running right away, curious to see what had happened, what kind of a Vein spirit Jacob was fighting, and if he and Fallon and Ray even needed help. It was the perfect opportunity for me to test myself without a magic shield keeping me locked, wasn't it? I had the pendant. It was time I put it to good use.

Maybe I would even get lucky, and this spirit would be just like the one in the alley. It would run off at the sight of me without my having to even give up control to the monster. That would definitely convince Jacob to take *me* while hunting spirits next time.

It had been a long time since I'd been so excited about a fight. Yes, this was exactly what I'd needed. What I'd *craved* since Jacob took me to his place. Gods, I'd missed it so much, my heart yearned.

Until I reached Jacob's truck and smelled the fire burning in the air. And I heard Jacob's voice.

"I did, as a matter of fact," he was saying.

I rushed my steps around the corner, between two houses across the street, and...I saw.

My breath caught in my throat. Every muscle in my body clenched, and I couldn't even hear my heart beating anymore.

It must have been a dream.

There was no way that I was looking at a burning house, and Ax standing in front of it while the flames licked his back. No way Jacob was there, too, together with Ray and Fallon.

He said *a spirit*. He was going after *a spirit*—not a vampire.

Most definitely not Ax.

"Last chance, Jacob. Tell me where she is, and I'll leave you alone."

The sound of his voice reached me like an echo. It filled my entire mind and body like magic, a *good* kind of magic, and my fangs were already extending. For a second there, reason didn't reach me. It was *him*. He was standing right there, dressed in a pair of ruined jeans, and a black leather jacket in even worse shape. He was bloody, bruised, and even though I was far away, I could still see his eyes. I could see the spark in them that had my body going weak. I could see that smile of his that turned my damned mind upside down. I could see *all* of him as if he was standing right there in front of me.

And my body craved him worse than blood. Even the whispers in my head were pushing me to just run, go to him, touch him, make sure he was real.

Make sure he was *here*.

But Jacob, Fallon and Ray were already raising their hands. The smell of magic overpowered everything else as their hands lit up with a glowing red light.

Ax didn't move. His smile widened and his arms raised as he prepared himself, but he didn't move.

If they hurt him again, I was going to fucking lose it. It didn't matter what he was doing here. It didn't matter why that house was burning, and why Jacob was after him.

I would *not* stand by and watch, everything else be damned.

I moved even before I realized it. My heart beat steady, my eyes locked on the magic, how fast it left their hands, the way it launched at Ax, and the asshole still wasn't moving. His eyes were locked on it, reflecting red as the magic drew nearer, and he was still there.

But so was I.

I didn't have the energy to even call for him to get the fuck down. My eyes were locked on him and my arms outstretched as I came at him from the side.

He turned his head at the last second.

I don't know if he saw my face or not, but he didn't have the chance to react. The heat of the magic coming for him almost burned the side of my face before I crashed onto Ax. My arms locked around him as we flew in the air, slamming against the ground, rolling at least three times before we stopped.

By then, an explosion shook the ground. Dark spots filled my vision, and the smell of magic overran that of the fire instantly. I was still breathing, my hands shaking as I made to stand up, still not seeing anything properly.

Hands on my face. Lips on mine.

I couldn't breathe.

My hands locked around his wrists and my eyes squeezed shut as if my body had forgotten that I actually needed air to survive. We never moved, never actually kissed, but we were there, breathing, our hearts beating.

And it occurred to me that I wouldn't mind being trapped right here for the rest of eternity.

When he let go of me and I opened my eyes, I could see his face in perfect clarity. Blood and grime coated his skin, but his eyes were just as alive as ever. Just as blue. Just as limitless.

"You're here," he whispered against my parted lips. "You're here."

So was he.

"Missed me, big guy?" I said breathlessly, so desperate to wrap my arms around him my knees were shaking.

But something moved to our side and the smile dropped from my face instantly. I turned, Ax's hands still on my face, to see Jacob, Fallon and Ray coming closer.

We'd ruined the fence of the house next door and we'd stopped right in the middle of the driveway. That nobody was coming out of their houses yet wasn't a surprise. I knew enough about magic now to know that everything was possible with the right spell.

It was just us out here, at least for now.

"Ax, let go," I whispered, trying to get his hands off me as I faced Jacob, but Ax wouldn't even look away from my face.

"Never," he whispered before he stepped behind me, wrapped an arm around my waist, the other gripping my hip. My body melted onto his chest on instinct. I had no fight left in me when it came to him. Just the way he held me knocked down all my defenses at once. Not that I had any left after not seeing him for so long.

But even so, I needed to stop Jacob and the others before they came closer.

"Nikki," Jacob said, and my name was a warning. His eyes were wide as he looked at me, confused, a bit angry.

"Don't come any closer," I told him, raising my hand.

Ax lowered his forehead to my shoulder as he held me, breathing deeply, heart beating a mile a minute. Did he even see that Jacob was still right there?

If he did, he couldn't care less.

It took all I had not to raise my hand to touch his head. Fuck, I'd almost forgotten what he did to me when we were close like that.

"I told you to stay back. *Why* are you here, Nikki?" Jacob demanded, and Ax held me tighter.

"Because you lied to me," I spit. "A Vein spirit? Really? A fucking Vein spirit?"

Jacob flinched, but he didn't even try to explain himself. "Step away from him, Nikki."

I thought for sure Ax would react. I thought he'd have something to say, at least.

Instead, he just kept kissing my shoulder, burying his face in my neck *right in front* of all of them, digging his fingers into my skin like he couldn't care less about anything in the world—not even death.

Fallon and Ray looked disgusted. Jacob looked positively terrified.

Meanwhile my body was about to fucking melt into a pile of goo in the ground.

"Ax," I hissed and tried to move away. He was fucking distracting me. I needed to be able to think, but he didn't let go. Instead, he just held me to him tighter.

"I'm not going to let you hurt him, Jacob," I said, and my voice shook. Too many emotions inside me. I felt like I was on a fucking roller coaster.

"He's a murderer," Jacob spit. "He has been killing sorcerers all over the country, Nikki. Almost twenty of them are dead in the past month."

"I would have killed more, but they kept waiting for me in big groups. That magic shit is nasty," Ax whispered in my ear, kissing my neck. "You smell like it. I need to change that asap."

"What the fuck, Ax?!" I growled, slamming my elbow in his gut, but he didn't move away a single inch.

"They wouldn't tell me where you were," was his response. He held me so tight for a moment, I was sure my ribs were bruised. "I thought you were dead, Damsel," he whispered.

There was so much pain in his words so suddenly, it nearly suffocated me. I felt all of it like it was mine. I felt his heartbeat and his warm breath blowing on my shoulder. I felt it in the way he held me, so desperately you'd think I was the only thing keeping him alive.

And it broke my heart. The anger was still there, but it was completely overrun by the pain that I momentarily forgot about it.

"Jacob, stop," I warned when he took yet another step closer.

"Told you we should skin her alive," Ray spit from behind him.

"Please don't do that," I warned because Ax was finally reacting. He *really* didn't like it when people talked about me.

"I would—" Ray started, but I cut him off.

"Don't fucking say another word!" I shouted.

Ax raised his head from my shoulder. "C'mon, say it," he told him.

"For fuck's sake!" I dug my fingernails into his knuckles until I drew blood. He still didn't let go of me—or stop.

"Don't listen to her. You're a big guy. You're tough. Just say what's on your mind. What would you do to her? You can tell me all about it," Ax said to Ray, and I could hear the grin in his voice perfectly.

"Jacob," I said, and Jacob raised his hand just as Ray opened his mouth again. He didn't make a single sound.

Thank the gods. "Look, I'll talk to him. He won't be killing anyone anymore—I promise you, okay? Just...just let me talk to him." All I needed was an hour.

Well. Maybe a couple. Three tops. Because let's face it—I was perfectly incapable of resisting his touch and his dirty mouth. So, there would be talking, but...there would be other things, too.

It was just until the sun came up, that's it.

"I'm afraid I can't do that, Nikki," Jacob said, and the fear, the confusion, were gone from his eyes. Raw determination reflected in them, and when he reached for his daggers, too, I knew there was no going back.

"Jacob, please," I whispered, pushing Ax back with all my strength. He finally gave just a little bit, and though he kept his hands on me still, there was an inch of space between us.

"You have a choice to make, Nikki," Jacob said. "I know you're not evil. I know you can do better than this. Remember the time we spent together." Behind me, Ax growled, and his fingers dug into my arms as he tried to pull me back, but I resisted. "He's a monster—you *know* that."

"I do," I whispered. I knew who he was perfectly. But... "He's *my* monster, Jacob." And I was his, no matter how fucked up the whole thing was.

"Rot in hell," Fallon spit, sticking her strange tongue out at me with a hiss. I ignored her.

"I can't let you hurt him," I told Jacob. "Just *please.* I'm begging you—"

"No," Jacob cut me off, and he raised his daggers at me. "This ends tonight."

The voices in my head had turned to screams. The monster wanted control so badly, but I gritted my teeth.

There was no way out of this, not without someone ending up dead. I didn't want that. I would not let Ax die, but I wouldn't hurt Jacob, either. I cared about him. He was actually a *good* guy. He'd taken care of me, and I refused to lay a hand on him.

I gave him my word. I would keep it until the day I died. I would help him just like he'd helped me.

But right now, the best I could do was whisper to Ax too low for anybody else to hear:

"Run."

Magic infused the air as the sorcerers raised their hands at us. Jacob had decided to chant out loud this time, too.

"I'm sorry," I told him, and I wished with all my heart that he saw I meant it.

Then, I turned around and ran with Ax right beside me.

CHAPTER NINE

We ran for two hours straight. I didn't know which direction we were going. I didn't really care.

But the sun was about to shine, and we needed a place to crash. I needed a place to *think*. I needed to make sense of this whole fucking night before it drove me nuts.

The whispers in my head no longer pushed me as hard as they had. I was *really* starting to love that pendant. And it just made me feel even shittier for running from Jacob like that.

It was all Ax's fault. The fucking lunatic. I couldn't even believe he was real. Who even goes around killing sorcerers like that without a fucking care in the world?

And why wasn't he even sorry?

I was going to murder him with my own damn hands.

We finally stopped at a roadside motel on a highway. Motorbikes were parked in the lot and there were at least thirty men in one of the rooms, listening to loud, heavy metal music and drinking. The scent of alcohol didn't even tempt me in the condition I was in.

We took a room on the second floor, and the words

were right there at the tip of my tongue, about to burst right out of me the second he opened the door.

"What the—"

That's as far as I made it. Ax pushed me against the wall, his lips on mine, his tongue deep inside my mouth.

A moan escaped me involuntarily. My traitorous body didn't care for reason or the fact that we *really* needed to talk. I wrapped my arms around his neck and pulled him to me even harder. He tasted of dirt and blood and so completely *Ax* that I was intoxicated before the second was over. Gods, I'd missed him even more than I realized. He touched me and I forgot there was a world out there. Sorcerers and magic couldn't reach me at all when he gripped me like that, like I was his lifeline, like he *lived* for me.

And I'd be a fucking liar if I said I didn't love every second.

We tasted each other, biting and sucking until my lungs demanded air again. His hands roamed down my back and he grabbed my ass, squeezing tightly before he slammed me to himself, and I felt all of his hard cock right on my stomach. I cried out, the need for him making my whole body shake.

"You smell like him," he growled, biting my neck as he grabbed my shirt. Without warning, he pulled it to the sides and tore it in half within a second.

"Don't fucking ruin my clothes!" I said, but it was Ax. I shouldn't have wasted my breath. The white bra I had on was in pieces on the floor next. Then his hands moved to the front of my shorts, and he pulled hard. The button fell and the zipper gave, before he grabbed them by the waistband and tore them off me, too. The fabric bit into my skin, but with him, the pain always added to the pleasure. He consumed me completely, and when he tore my panties off, too, he stopped to breathe for a second, his forehead pressed to mine.

"I'm going to wipe that scent off you, Damsel," he said, breathing heavily, before he pulled me up. My legs locked around his hips instantly, and I held onto his neck as I licked his lips. Fuck, the taste of him was otherworldly. I hadn't even realized it, but I'd been starving for it. My back hit the bed and he fell on top of me, never loosening his arms. The pressure of his body on mine set my skin on fire.

"You're *mine*. You can only ever smell like me," he growled before he bit my bottom lip hard enough to draw a bit of blood.

"I'm *not* yours," I said, but he knew I was a fucking liar.

That's why his lips stretched into a grin as they hovered over mine.

"Do you have any idea how long I've waited for this?" he whispered that sexy sound that had my insides melting. Fuck, I'd missed the sound of him, too.

"Umm…a month?" I said breathlessly.

He grinned wider. "A fucking lifetime."

His hand moved lower, and he raised himself up a bit, before he brought it between my legs. My eyes squeezed shut when his middle finger slipped down my soaking wet folds. I moaned and threw my head back as the pleasure consumed me. It wasn't fair how fast he got me there. He bit my chin, growling, and teased my entrance with his fingertip.

I was already a goner.

"Ax," I begged, thrusting my hips up, but he didn't let me. He loved to torture me before he gave me mind-numbing pleasure, but I wasn't in the mood for games right now. I needed him too much. I was fucking starved for him.

"Fuck, Damsel," he whispered, unwrapping his arm from around me and pulling up to his knees between my legs. He analyzed every inch of me, and the more he saw, the more in awe he looked. I never felt more *seen* than when he looked at me, when he touched me. And the more of it I felt, the more I realized just how much I'd forgotten in the month we'd been apart. Just how much I'd *chosen* not to think about, in hopes it would make being away from him a bit easier.

But there was no choosing now. I felt all of it and it broke my heart just as fast as it set my body on fire.

Slowly, he took his jacket off, showing me his naked torso, every scar on his skin, every curve of his muscles. I knew all of it by memory now, even if I didn't want to admit it. I ached to run my hands all over him.

"Look at you," he breathed as he undid the zipper of his jeans. I held my breath, eyes locked tightly on him, and when he pushed those jeans down, he showed me the object of all my fantasies.

How many times had I touched myself while I'd been away, imagining his cock inside me? How many times had I come, whispering his name, for fear somebody at the house would hear me if I'd screamed it like I'd wanted to?

I'd lost count the first week.

And when he grabbed his cock in his hand and started to stroke himself slowly, I almost came at the sight alone. He looked like a fucking god.

I made to touch him, but he grabbed my wrist lightning fast and stopped me.

"Don't you fucking dare," I warned, and it only made him smile more.

"I need to have my way with you," he whispered,

lowering himself over me slowly. "I won't be done until every inch of you smells like me. Do you understand?"

"I just saved your life. The least you can do is fuck me when I ask you to," I said, and he threw back his head, laughing. Even though I *really* didn't want to give in, it was impossible to hold back a smile when he laughed. It was rough and sexy, and it vibrated throughout me, but more than that—it was *honest*. Like he really hadn't heard anything funnier in his life. Everything he did with me, he *meant* it. There was no second-guessing with him.

"I'll get to that part, Damsel," he whispered, biting my bottom lip. "I'll do it *slowly* because I love the sound of you begging for my cock."

Taking his upper lip in my mouth, I sucked hard until I was sure it hurt, but he just moaned instead.

"I won't beg," I lied. We both knew I would.

"Let's see, shall we? Let's prove you're a liar," he said with that awful grin that had my heart racing. He fell on top of me, knocking the breath out of my lungs. My limbs locked around him instantly, and I pulled him to me with all my strength.

"My greedy little slut," he whispered, licking my neck, sticking his tongue in my ear. His hand moved lower, under my thigh, and he pressed two fingertips to my entrance. I cried out, my eyes squeezed shut as I waited...

"You're so fucking wet for me, Damsel," he whispered, teasing my folds. "You want this?" He let go of my pussy, grabbed his cock in his hand and brought the tip to my entrance.

I pulled him with all my strength, and raised my hips, too, but it was useless. He wouldn't budge. Frustrated, I sank my fingernails in his back, and he moaned louder.

"You want my cock?"

"Yes," I breathed.

"Tell me you're mine, baby," he whispered, running his tip through my folds as he growled. I could feel the muscles on his back clenching as he held himself from thrusting inside me, the jerk.

"Fuck you," I hissed and tried to pull him to me again.

"Oh, I will. I'll fuck you so hard you won't remember your name. I'll fuck you so thoroughly you won't ever get the feel of my cock out of your pussy," he breathed, pressing onto me harder. "I'll fuck you so long there won't be any other scent on you but mine."

"Big talk," I whispered, about to come just by the feel of his tip on my folds. "Why don't you show me instead?"

He bit my jaw with a growl. "I will, but I need to know that you know who you belong to first."

He thrust himself inside me only halfway. My back arched and my eyes squeezed shut. I swear I saw stars. The way he filled me up was something else.

But he moved back just as fast.

"Myself," I said, already high on pleasure.

"Who do you belong to, Damsel?" he whispered, teasing me with his fingers again.

I fucking loved the games we played, but I was about to explode for real.

"Ax, please," I begged, just like he knew I would.

"Who does this pussy belong to?" He stuck his middle finger all the way inside me.

My eyes rolled in my skull. One small movement and I was going to come. I held onto the feeling tightly, waiting for the bliss, but...

He took his finger out of me instantly, making me cry out.

"Who—"

"*You!*" I hissed, digging my fingernails into his shoulders. "I belong to you, asshole. If you don't—"

But he didn't let me finish. He stuck his tongue in my mouth and kissed me furiously, his fingertips on my pussy, playing with me the way only he knew how. He moved lower, tracing kisses down my neck, my chest, until his face was right in front of my breasts. When he bit my nipple, my back arched all the way. I held him by the back of his head to make sure he *never* let go. He sucked and licked and bit every inch of my breast like a real savage. I loved that he was so rough, that he didn't give me enough time to even breathe properly. I loved that his fingers dug into my thighs, probably bruising me in the process. I loved that he knew exactly when to let go of my nipple before positioning himself in front of the other.

His fingers thrust inside me all the way without warning. It was a miracle my body hadn't collapsed yet.

"Come for me, Damsel," he ordered, then took my nipple in his mouth and sucked hard, while his fingers pumped in and out of me fast.

I lasted about three seconds. If whatever he did to me wasn't magic, I don't know what was.

But even though I was still high on the aftermath of the orgasm, Ax wasn't done. My eyes were closed and my heart beat so fast, it felt like it shook my whole body. He'd meant it when he said he wanted to fuck me *thoroughly*. His fingers had been first. Now, as he dipped his head between my thighs, I had no doubt that he was going to keep torturing me before he gave me release again. And I had the feeling he wasn't going to let me even *touch* him tonight.

He wanted to mark me. He wanted to coat me in his scent. He wanted to *own* me.

And I was perfectly happy to be owned.

CHAPTER
TEN

His teeth made a mess out of my thighs. My skin was raw red, but the pain barely registered. I was propped up on my elbows, unable to look away from him as he feasted on my pussy like he meant to lick every drop off me. I moved my hips in rhythm with his tongue, so desperate to feel it all the way inside me.

"Ax," I breathed, but he refused to raise his head. He just kept going furiously, like eating me was the purpose of his life.

"Ax!" I tried again, and he finally looked up at me and let go of my folds.

"Don't interrupt me while I'm eating, Damsel," he said with a growl, and dove in again like a mad man, licking and sucking and biting until my own arms gave up on me, and I fell on the bed, breathless. My hips moved, my whole body clenching as the pleasure built up inside me.

He knew *exactly* when to stick his fingers in me. He knew exactly when to suck on my clit, how fast I needed it, how rough. That's why, when *he* wanted me undone, I came, screaming out his name until my throat burned. The pleasure consumed me completely. I was weightless, floating in the air, mind blank and heart full, a lazy smile on my face.

I wanted to be here forever, but...

"I need you here with me again."

My eyes opened to see his face right in front of mine as he licked my juices off his swollen lips. I moved up and grabbed the bottom one between my teeth, sucking hard. He moaned, thrusting his hips against me, his throbbing cock right on my pelvis.

"There you are," he said, invading my mouth with his tongue for a moment.

I tried to move my hands lower, to grab his cock and position it to my entrance because I was already yearning for it. It didn't even surprise me anymore—it's just how it was with him. I was insatiable. I was *mad,* and I didn't even feel bad about it. I just wanted to take everything he could give me all the damn time.

"I want to touch you, too," I said, too tired to even try to sound angry.

"I know, baby," he whispered. "But if you do, I won't last. And you feel so fucking good when I please you."

"You *will* please me." I always lasted way less than him. And then I licked his lips. "Baby, *please.* Don't make me wait," I whispered in my girliest voice. I batted my lashes at him, too.

And it was ridiculously easy to do.

His face changed instantly. His eyes were even more on fire, and he moved back just for a second, before he thrust himself inside me all the fucking way with one swing.

Oh, *yes.*

I cried out as he growled like an animal. It took a little while to adjust to the size of him, even now. We both needed a second, but when the air returned to my lungs, I grinned.

"Weakling," I whispered, and he was surprised. It had been so easy to mess with him. *Baby, please* and he caved. Valuable information to have.

But Ax grinned, and then he buried himself even deeper inside me. I didn't even know it was possible, but I was so full of him, I lost control of my body completely.

"I am, Damsel," he growled. "I'm a fucking puppy when it comes to you."

His every word rang true, and it filled me in a different way, until I was sure I'd melt away for real. He held my eyes as he moved back, then thrust himself inside me again, even harder than the first. My mind was already not my own, and with each new thrust, I was a bit more gone. His hand closed around my neck as he fucked me, never even blinking his eyes.

"You haven't been with anybody else," he whispered against my lips.

"How would you know?" Of course, I hadn't been with anybody else. Who in the world could come even close to this man? The way he felt right now, sliding in and out of me—*nobody* could compare.

"I know your pussy," he said. "I know how tight you are."

My eyes rolled in my skull when he thrust inside me again. Fuck, he felt so good.

"Maybe I just fucked someone with a smaller dick," I teased breathlessly, and his hold around my neck tightened again.

He growled in my ear. "Don't tempt me, Damsel."

"Or what?" I choked. The way the pain collided with the pleasure in my body was incredible. It was all I could do to hold myself back as he pounded into me over and over again.

He raised his head up, grinning. "Or you'll be begging for my cock in vain."

"Empty threats," I whispered, holding onto his shoulders. I was so, so close...

Ax stopped moving. "Do you wanna try me?"

"No!" Fuck that, I didn't want to try anything right now.

"Good girl," he whispered, then continued to fuck me until I came for the third time.

It lasted a long time, and he didn't let go of me, didn't stop digging his fingers into my skin, or pumping in and out of me until he let go, too.

And I wondered, how had I ever lived my whole life without him? How had I survived without *this*?

It was more than just a release—it was freedom. And as I came down to earth again, there was absolutely no doubt in my mind that I was *never* going to leave his side again.

I was so screwed.

"Come here."

I pretended I couldn't hear him and hugged the pillow tightly. The sun was up, and my body was exhausted, my mind too caught up in the pleasure to think about what awaited me at nightfall, thank the gods.

"Damsel, come here," Ax said again from the other side of the bed.

And when I didn't move, he grabbed me, just like I knew

he would. Just like he had last time we'd slept together. Only this time, I had no fight left in me. I just settled on his shoulder, the most comfortable place I'd ever laid on in my life. I fit him perfectly, so it was easy.

My eyes were closed, and unconsciousness was seconds away. For the first time in my life, I wanted to hold on, *not* fall asleep, just for a little longer.

Fuck, he messed with my mind in so many ways it wasn't even funny.

"I thought I lost you," he whispered so low, I was afraid I made it up. I was too far gone to even open my eyes, let alone speak. His own damn fault for being so comfortable. The heat of his skin was everything I needed and never even knew.

"I don't know where you were or what you did, but even if you chose to be away from me, I hope you never make that choice again."

He sounded more like he was talking to himself than to me. I could barely hear him, but his words broke my heart. The pain in his voice cut me wide open.

He thought I had died. How? Had he seen it when those sorcerers had thrown a house on my head, then set it on fire? Wasn't he supposed to be on his way to the Realm with Marie and her brother by then?

I wanted to tell him not to worry. I hadn't *chosen* to be away from him—I'd chosen to do whatever it took to be with him, even when I didn't know for sure that that's what *he* wanted. I didn't really think he'd meant it *literally* when he said he'd burn the whole Realm to the ground to be with me, but now I knew that he did.

Ax Creed was *not* a good guy—at least not to the rest of the world. He was a monster, a villain…and there was no need to second guess anymore—he was all *mine*. It was incredible how much power knowing that gave me.

Tomorrow, I'd tell him all about it.

Tomorrow, I'd tell him that I would burn down the whole world for him, too.

CHAPTER
ELEVEN

THE WHISPERS WOKE ME UP. AS SOON AS MY EYES OPENED, I FELT a bit *cold*, right there on my chest. Like something was missing.

And I knew exactly what.

I sat up with the jolt, looking down at my chest. *Empty* chest. The pendant was gone.

My heartbeat doubled instantly. Without it, even the whispers in my head were getting stronger. I didn't remember taking it off last night—I *wouldn't*.

So, where the fuck was it?

As soon as I looked to the right, I found it on the nightstand next to the bed. I'd never grabbed something or put it around my neck faster in my life. And the moment I felt the silver pressed to my skin, I began to relax. It wasn't lost. It was right here, where it should be. I could breathe much more freely right away.

The door on the left of the room opened, and I turned to see Ax walking out of the bathroom, skin wet, a white towel wrapped around his hips. All thoughts of the necklace and the whispers faded away from my mind just like that, and he became the center of my attention. The asshole took my breath away and had my mouth dry instantly. I hated his guts for it, but there was no way I could hide it. He always knew how to catch me off guard—and the worst part was that he didn't even have to try.

He saw my reaction perfectly, and he *loved* it. That's why he grinned. The night before came back to me in a rush. Those things he'd said to me while I slept in his arms. It was almost *romantic,* which made me want to gag, obviously.

But believe it or not, a part of me actually *liked* it. A very, *very* small part of me, but still.

My lips stretched into a smile before I even realized it, and my body was already starting to heat up, knowing what he'd want to do—be inside me, right now. And for a second, nothing else mattered again. Just like that.

Like I said: *magic.*

But then he looked down at my chest and he saw my pendant.

Ax's smile dropped instantly, and he even stopped walking. "Take that thing off."

Shocked for a moment, I raised my brows. "Good evening to you, too."

He leaned his head to the side. "Take it off, Damsel."

What the... "No." Was he serious?

"It smells like him," he spit, suddenly angry. And I knew he meant Jacob.

Fisting my hands tightly, I raised my chin. "Well, he had it made for me, so..."

The next second, he was on the bed with me. "Take it off." This time it was a damn warning, too.

Anger infused my blood instantly. I saw red. "Fuck you, asshole. You're not the boss of me."

He moved almost too fast for me to even notice and wrapped his hand around the back of my neck. He pulled me closer until the tips of our noses touched. "I can't fucking stand the smell of him on you."

His eyes were so dark they barely looked blue anymore. He was actually *serious* about this, and it just pissed me off even more. The pendant didn't even smell like Jacob—it smelled like *magic*. But turns out, he was a jealous psycho, and it wasn't my fucking problem.

I pushed his hand away and stood up, not even caring that I was completely naked. "Well, that's too bad because I like it. I'm going to keep it." And just because he was being a dick about it, I wasn't going to tell him shit.

I made to move for the bathroom, but he was in front of me before I could blink, looking down at me like he was both in pain and batshit crazy at the same time.

Crossing my arms in front of me, I raised a brow. "What?"

"He fucking *marked* you with his magic," he growled.

"He didn't."

"Yes, he did. And you're choosing to keep it on you, even now." He came closer. "Why?"

"Because I like it," I spit. In fact—I *loved* that thing and what it did to help me keep control. No way was I going to give it up. And I would tell him about it, too, just as soon as he stopped being an asshole.

"Fuck, Damsel," he said through gritted teeth. "Why didn't you come to find me? Where the fuck were you with him? What were you doing?"

Accusations—all of them. I could hardly believe it, but he looked me dead in the eye and fucking *accused* me like he really thought he was my maker.

"None of your damn business," I spit, so angry I couldn't see straight.

Lucky for me, I did see enough to move past him and into the bathroom, slamming the door shut behind me with all my strength.

Who the hell did he think he was, talking to me like that? What did he think I was doing out there, fucking every guy I saw? And even if I did do exactly that, it wasn't his damn business.

Gods, he pissed me off so much I could barely breathe. The cold shower didn't help, not even when I heard him walking out of the motel room, slamming the door behind him. Where was he even going? Because we needed to move. I had a plan and I needed to see it through before I could even think about doing any of this with him.

When I walked out of the bathroom, I remembered that he'd torn all my clothes that Jacob had gotten me the night before.

"Goddamn prick," I muttered to myself, right before I noticed the flowery scent spreading in the room. There were two plastic bags right by the bed that hadn't been there when I woke up.

I went to inspect, only to find them full of clothes. Clothes...*for me.* Two skirts, flared up just like I liked them, four crop tops in different colors, black leather boots, a brand new cropped leather jacket, three pairs of panties and a bra—all lacy and black.

Fuck, the fabric was so soft. These clothes were brand new, the tags still on them, and the second I put on the panties, I knew everything would fit me perfectly. They all did, even the bra.

And I felt more like myself than I had in a really long time.

But when I stepped in front of the mirror, the smile vanished. Because now I felt like *shit*, too, for lashing out at him like that. Too many things happening all at once. I was afraid and excited and so fucking *happy* to be with him again, and I had no idea how to even react to it all. How to be *normal* without being hateful toward him.

I heard his footsteps and smelled his scent a second before he came into the room again. I walked out of the bathroom, determined to suck it up and just *talk* to him. We were both adults. We could have a normal fucking conversation together.

But he was there, dressed in new clothes himself—a new pair of dark wash jeans, a new jacket, and even a white *shirt* underneath it. I'd literally never seen the guy with a shirt on, and it looked fucking hot on him, the way it showed just enough of his curves without being too tight.

I was already drooling.

His eyes scrolled down the length of me slowly, and they lit up just like always. I'd be a liar if I said I didn't love knowing how hungry he was for me at any given moment. And now that I was wearing *his* clothes and I smelled like him after last night, he should be happy. He shouldn't be so pissed off.

Instead...

"We're leaving," he said, nodding his head back at the door.

Don't get mad. "Leaving where?"

"Home. We're going back home," he said, like there was no room for arguing with that statement at all.

I felt my own lips stretch into a wicked smile. "I am not going home."

He looked like I slapped him across the face. "Yes, you are. We're not safe out here."

"Okay, then, if you're afraid, go ahead. I won't stop you." I crossed my arms in front of my chest and held his eyes.

His jaw was going to break by how tightly he clenched his teeth. "Damsel," he whispered.

"You *do not* get to order me around, Ax," I said, and I tried my best to keep my voice calm. "I am *not* going back home. I *can't* go back home."

"Where else do you want to fucking go?" he roared, stepping closer to me. "What—you want to go back to your fucking sorcerer?"

Oh, gods, this was getting old already.

I burst out laughing. "You asshole!" I spit, stabbing him in the chest with my finger. "Did it even occur to you to *ask* how I am, where I was, what happened to me, how I even survived? Did you think to sit down with me like a normal person and *talk* to me?" That wasn't too much to ask, was it?

"I would have if you didn't keep *his* mark on you willingly!" he spit. "You fucking disappeared! I thought you were dead, but no—you were alive and well, hiding out here with Jacob fucking Thorne while I lost my fucking mind trying to find you!"

"I didn't know that you thought I was dead, okay?! I didn't fucking know that you were out here killing people to find me!"

Suddenly, he grabbed my face in his hands. "Liar," she whispered. "You knew. I told you I would. You *knew*."

"Ax," I whispered, hating to see all that pain in his eyes, knowing I'd caused it.

"Answer me one thing honestly," he said. "*Could* you come back? Was it possible for you to come back to me in all this time I've been searching for you?"

Oh, gods. Jacob had never forbidden me to go out. I'd chosen to stay in because of the fear of what I'd find on the other side of those walls, afraid I'd lose control, just like always. Afraid I'd do something I'd regret. Instead, I'd stayed in and I'd hoped against all odds that I would be able to control my spirit on my own, or even that Jacob would get tired of trying eventually and just take me to whatever monster he wanted dead, so that I could finally be free of that stupid fear.

Holding Ax's eyes, I swallowed hard. "Yes." There was no point in lying to him because he'd know.

He smiled so bitterly, my knees shook. "Ax, wait—"

"I'll be outside. You can lead the way when you're ready."

He let go of me and was at the door before I could blink.

He slammed it shut behind him, and I stood there and watched it with my mouth wide open for a good five minutes, not knowing what to even think.

What the hell is happening?

Arizona. That's where I was headed. It would take about twenty hours to get there by car. If we were careful and ran most of the way, we'd get there in two nights. Assuming we didn't run into trouble.

Which would be foolish of me. Jacob wasn't just going to let it go. He'd come after me, I knew he would.

I never intended to break my oath. I swore that I would help him fight whatever he was up against, and I would. I suspected that was even the reason why I wasn't drawn to him in the first place, after making that blood oath. My word meant something. I was going to keep it. The magic of the oath had no reason to turn on me.

I'd just keep my word *alone*, without Jacob. We never said that we needed to be *together* to finish whatever he wanted gone. That wasn't part of the oath. And when I killed whatever was in Arizona, I'd find him. He'd set me free, and we'd have no business together for the rest of our lives. Exactly as it should be.

The Tonto Park had been circled three times in red on that map I saw on his desk. I hadn't even asked him because I knew he wouldn't tell me, but it was an easy guess that the Vein spirit he wanted gone was there. Or Vein *spirits*. Either way, I could take them on my own. I didn't need his help, not with what lived inside of me.

Right now, though, I couldn't help but be angry at the dickhead who refused to even look at me as we walked down the crowded street. We were in Des Moines, and in another couple of hours, we'd make it out of the city, run the highway and hopefully get all the way to Colorado by sunrise. From there, we'd run straight to Arizona.

"Did you get them there safe?" I asked after at least an hour had passed. The curiosity was too much. As much as I didn't want to talk to him at all right now, I wanted to know.

Ax kept his eyes ahead, never even turning toward me.

"Yes." His voice was perfectly emotionless. It bothered me more than was reasonable.

"Are they safe now?"

"They are."

I squeezed my eyes shut, breathing deeply. "*Where* are they?"

"In my house."

"Did they tell you why they sent us after Marie?" I tried again.

"No."

That was as much as I could take. "For fuck's sake, just *look* at me!"

A couple passing us by looked at us like they were *disturbed* by my shouting. It took all I had not to flip them off.

Ax finally turned his head toward me. No spark in his eyes. No emotion on his features, either. "What?"

That's it. That's all he had to say to me—*what*.

"You *really* want to do this?" I hadn't seen him in a whole month, and he wanted to be jealous of a fucking necklace?

"Do what?"

My ears rang. I don't think I'd ever been more frustrated in my life.

Fuck this. I could stop by a butcher's shop while we were in the city. It was still early. And after I was full of blood, I could buy myself a nice big bottle of vodka, too. There was enough space for it in the plastic bag with my new clothes hanging on my wrist. I didn't have to feel like this, did I? I could just drown myself in alcohol until sunrise.

"Never mind," I said with a sigh and stopped walking. This was already exhausting. I couldn't even stay mad anymore. Too much. "I'm on my way to Arizona, and—"

"Why Arizona?"

"Because." I let that sink in for a second. "I need to make it to Colorado tonight, then take it from there tomorrow. You don't need to come with me," I told him. "In fact, I'd much rather make the way myself. And when I'm done,

I'll be back in the Realm. If you want to talk then, we will. If not..."

I stepped back, feeling like I'd just swallowed a sack of rocks. Something must have been wrong with me. If I wasn't a vampire, I'd go see a fucking doctor because I felt sick.

Ax laughed like he'd just heard the funniest joke of his life.

"You're not going anywhere without me," he whispered, shoulders still shaking, and it sounded like a warning.

I should have been pissed off about it, not *relieved*. I should have held my ground, pretended I didn't want him with me, not *force back a stupid smile*.

"Then stop acting like a five-year-old," I said, but it didn't sound half as bitter as I meant it.

He came closer, looking at my lips like he wanted to bite them off completely. Shivers rushed down my back instantly.

"Take it off," he ordered in barely a whisper.

Aaand I was angry again. Great.

"*No*," I spit, then turned around and crossed the street without warning.

He'd follow. Of course, he would. Despite everything, he wasn't going anywhere. *Thank the gods*, as pathetic as that made me feel.

"I've got time, Damsel. I'll wait," he called after me but kept a good distance, for which I was glad. I didn't understand why I even let him get under my skin like that. But the way he *ordered* me around made me see red. In bed, that was fine. More than fine—I loved pleasing him. But out here? No fucking way.

"Screw you, asshole," I called, and people around me

stared. This time, though, I couldn't keep myself in check. "What the hell are you looking at?!"

Their heartbeats sped up instantly as they moved their eyes away from me. I heard their blood rushing, calling out my name like a siren song. I really needed that blood. And that vodka.

And I must have been in luck because just as I turned the corner, I saw a butcher's shop on the other side of the intersection.

Now, I just needed to get around back and steal some blood, and I'd be good as new.

"It's cold. It's disgusting," Ax said from behind me as he stared at the shop, too.

"It's blood," I said, and as soon as the streetlight turned green, I crossed the street. Then I continued to walk, searching for an alley close to it that would lead me to the back.

"What are you doing?" Ax called from the street corner. "It's *that* way."

I rolled my eyes. "I know, asshole. I don't have money. I need to steal it."

"I'll pay if you ask nicely."

I flipped him both birds. "Rot in hell."

But by the time I turned around, he had materialized right in front of me, which I already expected. I was used to the way he moved by now. Most vampires didn't bother—too much energy spent when we moved so fast. But Ax seemed to have plenty of energy to spare.

"It's a waste of time to go stealing right now. Just ask nicely," he said.

"Screw you."

"You did—just last morning," he said, but at least he

was back to being amused. I didn't get why I loved that look on him so much. It just got to me.

"It was a pity fuck. You were so desperate to find me, I felt sorry for you."

His smile widened. "Is that what it was?" he said as he leaned closer. I bit my tongue to keep from smiling. "You felt *sorry* for me?"

"Mhmm."

"You're feeling sorry for me now, too?" he said, then licked my lips so fast, I barely felt his tongue. The hair on the back of my neck stood at attention instantly. The way I was turned on now left no room for anger. As much as I hated him for *that*, too, I also liked it. A little bit.

"Very. You're just so pathetic, it's sad," I said, raising on my tiptoes to grab his lip between my teeth. Fuck, he tasted so good. We could go back to being angry—in a second. A little taste never hurt nobody.

"You know what's even more pathetic?" he breathed against my lips, and his hands closed around my naked waist. He squeezed until my lungs were completely empty, and I had no complaints whatsoever. "I can make you beg me to fuck you right here in the street, Damsel. I can make you get on your knees in front of all these people and choke on my cock, then ask for more."

My thighs were clenching so hard, my knees shook, because he was absolutely right. I was *this* close to grabbing him and taking him somewhere dark.

"So, so sad," he whispered, and his voice alone had my stomach twisting. I wanted to kiss him so badly. Grabbing him by the jacket, I raised on my toes again, my mind halfway gone, and he...

Stepped back.

He looked down at my skirt and raised his brows.

"You're dripping, Damsel. That must be *really* uncomfortable. C'mon, let's go." And he turned around and walked down the street to the butcher's.

I stared after him with my mouth open. *Again*.

He did not just walk away from me like that. He was hard—I *saw* the bulge in his jeans! He wanted to kiss me. He *never* held himself back from taking what he wanted from me.

So, what the hell was he doing?

Trying to get my body to cool down wasn't working, and those damn wet panties sticking to my folds were making me uncomfortable for real. I don't know why I was so surprised—it was Ax. He just *had* to have the last say. He loved his games, I knew that perfectly by now.

And so did I.

Which was why, the moment he stepped out of the butcher's shop with a plastic cup in his hand full of blood, I dropped the bag on the ground and slowly brought my hands under my skirt.

Ax stopped walking. His lips parted as he watched me take off my panties right there in the middle of the sidewalk. Whether people watched me or not didn't matter. I only had eyes for him.

My gods, the look on his face was priceless. I *lived* for those moments when I beat him at his own game.

Holding back a laugh, I threw the panties away behind me.

Ax disappeared from my view, and I found him crouched over as he caught my panties just before they hit the ground. Some of the cold cow blood in the cup spilled all over his hand.

"You're the fucking devil," he breathed as he straightened up, but his lips stretched into a smile, too.

I grabbed the cup from his hand.

"Let me help with that." Bringing his hand to my lips, I licked off every drop of blood between his fingers, all the while holding his eyes. The city didn't exist. The entire world faded away, too. It was just us in the entire universe. And when I brought his middle finger in my mouth, and sucked a bit too harshly, a moan left his parted lips, making me drip even more.

Forcing a grin on my face, I let go of him and stepped back.

"Thanks, big guy." With the cup in my hand, I turned around and walked away while he stared after me, unable to move for a good long minute.

Chapter

TWELVE

I WAS HOPING TO MAKE IT TO DENVER, BUT WHEN WE REACHED Sterling, we only had an hour until sunrise. So, it was best we stopped there for the day. The city was quiet at that time of night, and I felt much more in control with that cold blood that Ax had gotten for me in my veins.

When I heard him walking the wide street behind me, I smiled at myself. He'd kept away the entire night as we ran in the fields and the highways, staying away from cities and towns as much as we could. So far, no trouble, which I counted as a blessing. If everything went the same tonight, I'd be in Arizona, and practically a free woman.

Right now, Ax didn't want to be near me because he knew what would happen if we talked again. We would do what we always did—fight, talk dirty until I got wet and he got hard, and then one of us would walk away because we had someplace to get to.

Except now.

We just needed to find a motel or an inn, and there was no other place to go for the rest of the day. There'd be a bed. We'd end up fucking each other's brains out, no doubt. And I was already looking forward to it. Being away from him for a month had been torture, but I'd managed because I hadn't had to actually *see* him, feel him, have him touch me the way only he knew how, listen to that sexy voice of his. But now that we were close to each other, it was worse. I craved him worse than blood.

"Let's stop here for the day," I said to the night, knowing he'd hear me.

"We still have an hour," he said from behind me.

I turned around, and he stopped walking, still ten feet away. "Afraid I'll bite?" I said with a grin.

He raised a brow. "Afraid I'll make you throw away those panties again."

I laughed. I had put on a new pair of panties as soon as I cooled off, and of course he'd smelled them on me. "You'll just carry them around in your pocket, too." And I winked.

He sighed, shaking his head, as if he had already given up. "And you'll need *water* to clean yourself up."

"Your tongue does a much better job at that."

"My tongue stays in my mouth."

Now, I was intrigued. Folding my arms in front of my chest, I smiled. "What are you gonna do—*stay away* from me until sunrise?"

"Precisely," he said, then continued walking.

"Are you serious?" Because he couldn't possibly be.

But he walked right past me, looking ahead like I wasn't even there.

"Ax!"

"There's a hotel over there. Let's get to it. We need the rest." And he didn't look back at me at all.

"Fine," I muttered, and with the stupid plastic bag in my hand, I followed him to the hotel. He didn't actually mean it—he was just bluffing. He'd change his mind as soon as we were alone. I was sure of it.

It was much fancier than the last motel we stopped in. This one had clean marble floors, nice low lights all over the lobby, and the bed was probably way more comfortable here, too. I already liked the citrusy scent hanging in the air, even the perfume of the guy behind the desk.

Until...

"We'll take two."

I was a couple feet behind Ax, just taking in the large lobby while he booked the rooms. I turned to him, pretty sure that I'd heard wrong.

Two? As in, two *rooms*?

"C'mon, let's go," Ax said, and without a single look my way, he took the cards and walked over to the shiny elevator doors, leaving me to stare after him.

Each time, I kept thinking *this* was it—the biggest surprise for the night, but no. He went and did it again every fucking second.

Speechless, I followed him inside the car, and he pressed the button to take us up to the third floor. The stupid music that turned on as soon as the doors slid closed was annoying, and he kept his eyes on the floor, hands folded in front of his cock as if he was afraid I'd grab it. We were in an elevator. I was pretty sure he'd fantasized about elevator sex—*who hasn't?* I was standing right there!

I looked at him, burned holes in the side of his face with my eyes, but he never once looked my way.

Wow.

It hurt my ego. Wasn't he the one always begging me to let him in?

"This is you," he said, offering me a white card, and he used his to open the door right next to mine in the narrow hallway. "Night, Damsel." He stepped inside and closed the door without looking at me at all.

My gods, he *meant* it. He actually really meant it. It wasn't a bluff.

Stunned still, I walked into my own room and dropped the bag on the floor. The room *was* nice, much nicer than I expected, the bed huge, the carpet lush, and the white and grey bathroom was perfect. Unfortunately, it all looked pretty damn dull in my eyes. I looked at the wall behind the bed in wonder. He was *right there*. I could hear his heart beating. I could hear him opening the bathroom door, then closing it behind him. Two seconds later, he turned the shower on, too.

He *wasn't* at my door yet.

"Fuck," I breathed. He really was going to stay away from me.

Fuck it. It wasn't the end of the world. I didn't *need* him, I just *wanted* him. There was a difference. And if he could act like a child, so could I. So, I stripped off my clothes, too, and got into the shower. I already couldn't wait for sunrise.

TIME CRAWLED JUST when you needed it to move faster. There was a nice silver clock on the fancy nightstand by the bed. My eyes were on the hands. I could have sworn those fuckers were moving in slow motion.

Meanwhile he was in his room on the other side of the wall over my head, heartbeat slightly elevated, blood rushing through his veins. I was so in-tune with his body, I could hear him better than most. Or maybe I was just too damn focused on him for my own good.

Twenty-five minutes until sunrise.

I sighed, pulling the blanket over my head. It smelled nice and clean, and it was soft, but I wasn't feeling it.

Pushing it aside, I went to the minibar across the room. I hadn't wanted to stop for alcohol because I'd have to steal, and Ax had been right—stealing was a waste of time. We'd been running most of the way here, too. But now, I wasn't going anywhere. I had time.

So, I grabbed a small bottle of vodka and lay on the bed again.

"Remember when we first met?" I said to the room, despite my better judgment. His heart skipped a beat at the sound of my voice. I smiled to myself, playing with the bottle in my hand. "You were so easy to get to. I hadn't had that much fun in ages."

I thought he wasn't going to speak to me at all. Pretend he was asleep. Just ignore me.

But he surprised me yet again.

"You just caught me off guard, that's all," he said, so slowly I barely heard it.

"No, you enjoyed it. I know you did." Just as much as me.

"I enjoy everything about you, Damsel," he said. "*Almost* everything."

"Come here," I said, before I could help myself.

"No."

Damn it. "Why not?"

"Because I'm so fucking pissed, I can't think straight," he admitted, and he hated himself for it. I heard it in his voice.

"Then use me," I said, eyes closed as I squeezed the unopened bottle. "C'mon. Use me and let it all out. We only have twenty minutes. Let's make them count." *I haven't seen you in a month, asshole,* was what I really wanted to say, but

I was terrified that he'd know just how much I'd missed him.

Why? I had no idea. But wherever that fear came from, it was too strong to resist.

Ax was silent for a long time.

"I know you're thinking about it," I whispered. "I know you want to be inside me right now."

No answer.

Fuck, it was really hard to breathe, and I was starting to panic. Just a tiny bit.

Licking my lips, I took in a deep breath, and...

"I still smell like Jacob Thorne," I said, my voice slightly shaking. I was playing with fire here, and it could go both ways. But I was a bit desperate now, and I just wanted him here. I couldn't fucking help myself. "I thought you said you wanted that smell off me."

"Damsel," he warned with a growl.

I sat up on the bed, heart beating a mile a minute.

"I'm just saying," I whispered. "If you don't get this smell off me, someone else will. All I have to do is go knocking on doors in this very hotel. Someone will answer. Then you'd have a lot of work to do getting *his* smell off me, too."

I swear, his heart didn't beat at all for a long second.

I thought for sure he'd move then. I thought he'd be in front of my door in the next second.

Instead, he just turned on his other side and stayed right there on his bed.

Half my mind was made up to do just what I said I would. Go knocking on doors until someone with a dick between their legs opened up—just to prove to him that I meant it.

Except...I didn't.

I didn't want a guy. I wanted *him*.

And now he knew I was full of shit, too.

Squeezing my eyes shut, I let the anger go. It would be useless. So what that he didn't want to be near me—I still had my fingers. Screw the vodka—I could use my hands.

And he would hear *all* of it.

So, pushing the blanket off me, I started touching myself. I'd gone to bed naked because I was *that* sure that he'd cave. Can't say I regretted it.

With my eyes closed, I imagined him hovering over me. I'd done it so many times while I was in Jacob's house, it came naturally to me now. I imagined the heat of his body searing me. His big hands were around my breasts, and when I squeezed my nipples, I imagined it was his teeth biting on them hard.

A moan left my lips as I moved my right hand lower, fingernails grazing my stomach, my legs spread out wide. My imagination was so vivid, I almost *felt* him pressed against my thighs for real as he ran his fingers between my folds, making me moan louder. I wasn't going to hold myself back. If he didn't want to be here, fine. He could stay in his room and sulk.

Meanwhile I teased my entrance with the tips of my fingers, picturing him in detail behind my closed lids. His cock was there instead, pushing against me, and when I slipped my fingers inside me, my hips rose as I cried out. It had been so long since I'd been able to do this without making a single sound, afraid the others at Jacob's place would hear, that the feeling was a hundred times more intense. My pleasure climbed as I moved my fingers in and out of me and imagined him pounding onto me violently. I bit my own lip and imagined him doing it. I dug my fingers into my thigh and imagined him doing it. I stuck my fingers in my mouth and sucked hard, imagining his cock there instead.

"Ax!" I breathed, so full of the image of him, of the sound of his moans that only existed on the inside of my head. I was so, so close... "Don't stop," I panted. "Don't st—."

The door burst open.

I sat up, heart in my throat, fingers drenched in my juices. He stood there in front of the broken door, looking like a man possessed. His eyes were bloodshot, and he breathed just as heavily as me. He wore his jeans, unbuttoned and unzipped, and nothing else.

I could see the tip of his cock perfectly, and my mouth watered.

He never looked away from me when he pushed the door closed. It wouldn't at first—he'd broken the handle, but he pushed it hard, and it finally fell in place. I didn't dare move for fear he'd realize he was here and change his mind. I just stayed there on the bed, legs spread, dripping for him.

I barely saw him moving, but the next second, he was sitting on the bed with me, his hand in my hair, pulling hard as he looked down at my parted lips.

"This what you wanted?" he growled. I'd never seen him look so *dangerous*, like a true mad man. It just added fuel to the fire burning me.

"Yes," I breathed. This was *exactly* what I wanted.

"You want me to use you like the little slut that you are?"

Oh, gods. "Yes." I tried to lean closer to his face and kiss him, but he pulled my hair down until I hit the pillow with a cry.

"I'll use you," he said, standing up for a second to take

his jeans off. A moan ripped from my throat at the sight of him naked. It was unfair how perfect he was. All those muscles, all those scars, paired with the hungry look in his brilliant blue eyes was going to be the death of me. "I'll make you pay for every time you fuck with my head." He grabbed me by the ankles and pulled hard until I was off the bed. My legs were shaking but he grabbed me by the waist and steadied me.

"Ax," I whispered, trying to wrap my arm around his neck. I needed to kiss him so badly.

But he didn't let me.

"If you don't obey each one of my orders, I'll stop," he told me, grabbing me by the neck while he came closer. "No games. No hesitation. I walk out."

Fuck. He meant it.

I nodded.

"Don't fucking nod—say it," he hissed.

"Yes," I said, so turned on I could come if he just kept holding me like that. Damn him. Damn him and my stupid body for loving everything about him, even more when he was being a possessive asshole. "I'll obey. Anything."

His face broke into a grin. It was a damn lethal weapon all on its own.

"That's a good girl," he whispered, then pushed me down. "On your knees."

Just the thought of his cock in my mouth had me trembling. He didn't let go of my neck. He squeezed harder instead as he held me back and grabbed his cock with the other hand. I was drooling as I watched him stroking himself. I tried to reach for him, too but he growled in warning, so I had no choice but to put my hand down.

"Spread your legs," he ordered, and I did so eagerly. "If you touch yourself, I walk out."

"But—"

I lost the ability to speak when his cock buried in my mouth all the way. The tip of him grazed my throat, and I moaned. Gods, I'd been fantasizing about this every fucking night. He didn't move away for a little while, instead tightened his fingers around my neck until I gagged. He loved the sound of it, and when he moved back, I wrapped my hands around the length of him, and took him in again. My tongue relished the feel of his skin, and I moved back and forth fast, fearing he'd stop me any second.

He didn't. Letting go of my neck, he threw his head back and moaned when I took him in all the way to the base again. My throat was already raw and my jaw hurt, but every second was worth it. The taste of him, the feel of him on my tongue was everything.

And when I started grazing him with my teeth as I went, just like I knew he liked, his hold on my hair tightened, and he pounded into my mouth harder. Fuck breathing—I could do this all day. I was so ready that I'd explode if I so much as flicked my finger over my clit.

But I didn't dare touch myself at all. If he stopped now, I was going to be miserable, and I couldn't take it.

He kept thrusting into me, and I used my teeth and my tongue to get from him everything I needed. The sounds he let out filled my head. My imagination could never even come close to the real Ax. He was just too intense. He didn't care if he hurt me—he knew I could take it. He slammed onto me over and over again. My saliva dripped on my chest, my naked thighs, and tears kept streaming down my eyes. My jaw was numb, but the taste of him on my tongue only got better with every thrust.

"Don't swallow," Ax ordered, pulling me to stop by the hair as he took his cock in his hand, and pressed the tip to my lips, outlining them. I let my tongue out to lick him, too, and he hissed as if I'd burned him. "Keep your mouth open and don't swallow."

He didn't give me the chance to respond before he thrust his cock in my mouth again.

I did as he asked.

When he came, he kept his eyes on me, burying so deep in my throat it hurt. His cum spilled all over my mouth and every instinct in my body demanded I swallow, but I didn't. I just let his cum slip out my mouth, until it dripped down my chin, onto my chest and thighs.

"Good girl," he whispered and pulled himself out of my mouth. "Don't move."

I didn't dare move a single inch as he stepped back a couple feet and looked down at me. His lips slowly stretched into a wide smile.

"Much better," he said, and when I looked down, I saw his cum was hanging onto the silver pendant on my chest.

I almost burst out laughing. I loved his possessiveness, despite the fact that it annoyed the shit out of me.

"Get up," he said, but he still didn't come closer. My legs were a bit numb from sitting like that for so long, but I didn't mind. "Get in the bathroom."

"Why?" There was plenty of space here in the room. The bed was here, too.

"Get. In," he growled, and as much as I wanted to jump him and slam him on the bed, I swallowed hard and moved for the bathroom. Did he want me to clean up? His cum was all over me. The taste of it coated my tongue, too. Salty and completely *Ax*. It fucking fried my nerve ends. How much longer was he going to make me wait?

He followed me to the bathroom, and when I turned to him, he just pointed at the sink. With a sigh, I went to it, looking at my face in the wide mirror. My gods, I hardly recognized myself. My cheeks were flushed, my eyes glossy from the tears, my hair all over the place. I looked *wild*, and the sight of a drop of his cum on my nipple made my thighs clench.

He stepped behind me, put his hand under my thigh and raised my leg. "Hands on the mirror," he whispered, and I leaned forward, touching the mirror with my palms. He grabbed my other leg, too, and pulled it up, until I was kneeling on the fucking sink.

"It's going to break," I warned. It was a big sink, and it was made of marble, but I wasn't sure if it could hold my weight.

"No talking," he said, running his hands down my back, digging his fingers into my skin just like I liked. My back arched instantly, and the mirror fogged up. "I want you to see everything I do to you with your own eyes. I want you to know what you look like when when I'm buried inside you. So fucking beautiful, Damsel," he whispered, then slapped my ass hard, making me cry out. "Don't let me catch you with your eyes closed." He moved his hands to my thighs, spreading them a little farther apart. "Not until you know without a shadow of doubt who you belong to."

His fingers moved up toward my pussy agonizing slowly. He took his time, staring at my face in the mirror, and he looked so damn fascinated by me, I really couldn't tell what he saw there.

What *I* saw was glazed eyes and flushed cheeks, parted lips raw red from friction. I was completely surrendered to him. My whole life hung on the movement of his fingers.

And when he pressed two against my clit, my eyes closed involuntarily.

Ax stopped touching me instantly.

I opened my eyes. "Accident! It was an accident!" I said, so panicked you'd think I was really about to die.

He grinned widely, his eyes lighting up. Then he pressed his fingers onto me again. My eyes remained open, even when he circled my entrance, then slapped my ass again hard. My eyes wanted to close, but I barely even blinked. The tip of my nose pressed to the mirror. He thrust two fingers inside me all the way, and my eyes opened wide.

They'd always looked cold. Colorless. Almost grey. But right now they looked *alive*. Full of color that almost seemed like it was *moving* as Ax fucked me with his fingers. The mirror fogged from my moans, and I had to clear it up so I could see the rest of my body, the way my hips moved in rhythm with his hand. The way my breasts bounced every time he thrust deep. The way my arms shook as I held onto the mirror.

Even more color added to my eyes as he picked up the pace. My face looked transformed with every new thrust, with every new level my pleasure reached. I'd never seen myself so alive before. The mirror had always showed me an image of a pissed off woman that was kind of scary. Never *this*.

And when Ax took his fingers out of me, I cried out in desperation. He couldn't stop now. I wanted it to last. I wanted to *see*.

But he fell down on his knees right behind me, and I saw him through the mirror, his face right between my legs. My breath caught when his tongue came out. I saw with perfect clarity when it licked my wet folds.

My entire body shook as I cried out, pressing my hips back onto him. His big hands gripped my thighs, and he squeezed hard. Just the sight of him grabbing me like that, with so much urgency, my pale skin red where his fingers dug into me, had me ready to let go.

But I gritted my teeth and I held back. I needed to see more.

And he gave me the show of my fucking life. I forgot to breathe as I watched him licking me, then stick his tongue inside me as far as he could. He ate me like he meant it. There was no holding back—he devoured me to pieces. I wanted to live right here in this moment for the rest of eternity, but I couldn't hold on a minute longer.

I looked up at my face, hoping to make it last just a bit more. And I saw exactly what he wanted me to see. It was written all over the blue of my eyes, the pink of my cheeks, my raw lips. I was undeniably his. My body belonged to him completely. So did my heart.

And my jaw was beginning to get really uncomfortable, too.

That's why I squeezed my eyes shut the next second and let go.

The pleasure made every cell in my body burst at the same second. It felt like I was no longer confined inside a body, but light as air, drifting into space.

And when I was aware of my surroundings again, I was no longer on the sink. I was in his arms and he lay me down on the bed gently.

Had the sun come out yet? Because I could barely keep my eyes open.

It had been too much. All my energy was now gone. And the mating instinct was back. I'd felt it in the way my fangs had wanted to come out of me. I'd felt it in my chest, too.

Did he know? Could he tell?

I'd die of embarrassment if he saw it.

But whether he knew or not didn't matter because he

didn't lay down on the bed with me. He just pressed his lips on my forehead and moved back.

I grabbed his arm but there was no strength left in me to hold him there. "Stay," I whispered.

Ax didn't say anything. He just left.

CHAPTER
THIRTEEN

Anya used to think that I was *strong*. I went through a lot and I was still here.

How would she know that I wasn't a coward instead? I was still here, but what state was I in? I used to constantly want validation from everyone. Always looking up to someone to make me feel better, to make life easier. And right now, I was pretty fucking convinced that what I'd had with Ezra had never been what I thought it was. I'd *forced* myself to feel for him. He was safe. He kept me grounded. He made me forget.

But it was *nothing* like what I felt right now. Like my heart was going to rip out of my chest soon if I kept going like this.

Nothing had ever felt like it. And that was probably why the mating instinct had never been awakened in me even after seven years.

With Ax, it had taken seven days.

And I didn't have the guts to even mention it to him, because...what if it wasn't the same for him?

I heard him when he was right behind the door to the

rooftop deck of the hotel. I'd come up here the second I'd heard him going into the bathroom in his own room. Yeah, *coward*. But I also knew he'd find me. All he had to do was follow my scent.

A second later, he opened the door and stepped outside.

The night was a bit cold, which suited me. The sky was dotted with brilliant stars, and the city around us was lively. The hotel was only seven stories, so we weren't that high. I could still see the people going about their business. The street lights. The car lights. The *life* being lived right under me.

They all seemed so free, I was jealous.

Ax came to stand beside me near the metal railing. His very presence was like a physical touch to my body, and now that I knew *exactly* what I looked like when he had his hands on me, it was impossible not to flush.

"How about now?" I said, trying to lighten the mood. "Do I smell like you?"

I saw it the second his face changed. Definitely the wrong question. Shit.

"Ax," I said, but he already moved back.

"No, actually. You smell completely like him. I could drench you in my cum and you would still smell like him," he said, a sickening smile on his face. "And you know what? Maybe it's a fucking sign." The blood rushing in my veins felt like lava already, but he kept going. "Maybe he made you *his* before I could. Maybe—"

That's as far as I could let him go.

"Fuck you, asshole! Nobody made me *his*!" I snapped.

And he kept walking backward to the door like he suddenly couldn't stand to be close to me. "So why the fuck do you keep his mark on you?!" he shouted.

"Because I *need* it!" I shouted back.

Fuck—how long did we last without shouting—*ten seconds?*

I turned back to the railing, eyes squeezed shut and hands fisted. He was going to walk away now, and we would go the whole night without even seeing each other, and then we'd end up right here again, as soon as we talked.

It was so damn exhausting. How much longer could we go on like this? It was impossible. Too much.

A long sigh escaped me, and I tried to let go of the anger because it was useless. Pointless.

And I needed the fucking whispers in my head to stop for a second.

When they did, I heard his heart still beating behind me.

I turned, shocked to see that Ax was still there. I thought he would be at least a mile away from me by now, but there he was. He had a fist pressed to the brick wall near the door and his head was down. He was breathing just as heavily as I was.

He hadn't left.

Closing my eyes, I took in a deep breath.

It was okay. We could do this, couldn't we? We were adults, for fuck's sake! We could have a normal fucking conversation without losing our shit.

He stayed. I could be calm, too. I could explain. He would understand. Wasn't that how this even worked?

Come to think of it, I'd never really argued with Ezra. He was never a jealous guy. He didn't care much about… anything, really. I used to joke and say I wanted to *be him* on my day off, just to put my brain on pause.

But Ax was different. Much different. And he probably never had to go through this with anyone before.

That didn't mean we couldn't learn.

"It stops the whispers in my head somewhat," I forced myself to say. My default setting was to be *angry* when forced to share something about myself, but I held it back. If it meant so much to him, I could tell him. I'd *never* told anybody about this before, even Jones, but I would tell him.

Ax turned to look at me, moving away from the wall, his expression unreadable.

"It helps me keep control of the...you know. The monster." I pointed in my chest. "It's a charm he had a friend of his make. It's supposed to take root in *my* mind and give *me* more control over my body."

"What whispers?" he said, squinting his eyes at me like he thought I was *lying* to him.

Do not get angry. Do not get angry, I reminded myself.

"The whispers. From the spirit," I said. "The...the Vein spirit that lives inside me."

Fuck, why was it so hard to say those words out loud?

"So, you've been touched," he whispered, and slowly started to come closer to me.

"Yeah. I mean, Jones thought so his whole life. I didn't really believe it because I'm a *vampire*, but apparently, it's true."

Shaking his head, he stopped a couple feet away from me. "But how?"

"I don't know. The spirit got to me first, while I was still human. Then I bit the vampire who was sucking the blood out of me, hence completing the turning process. And then I turned, and the spirit stayed with me. Somehow." I flinched. "I don't fucking know, to be honest."

His brows shot up. "You...turned *yourself*?"

"Yep. Pretty much." I was a kid. And I wasn't *me* at all—

I was the monster in those moments. It was just using my body.

"Explain how it whispers to you," he said, but he wouldn't come closer. He wasn't mad. He wasn't even judging me; he was just curious. More than that—he *needed* to know. And as much as I didn't want to tell him more, I still did it.

"It's just voices. They whisper, they scream. Sometimes it feels like one, sometimes like several," I said. "I don't know, they're just all over my head. They push me, and when I lose control and they take over, I turn into that thing you saw that night."

For a long second, Ax just looked at me. He didn't smile, he didn't tease, he wasn't angry yet—he just watched me.

And when he had enough, he was in front of me, his hands on my face. I leaned into them, so willing to surrender it was ridiculous. It felt like I was someone else completely right now.

"Why do you need that thing to control it?" he whispered, bringing his forehead to mine.

"Because I can't do it myself. I've been trying. Every single day since I went with Jacob. I've been trying, but it's useless. The spirit is too powerful."

"That's bullshit," he said without missing a beat. "You don't need that thing. You are strong enough to control it on your own if you just focus. If you stop drinking, and—"

"Stop it," I hissed and moved back, away from his touch. "Don't you think *I've tried?* I've been sober since that fucking night, and what do I have to show for it? *Nothing*!" I pulled the silver pendant out from under my shirt, and he looked away. "This slows the whispers down. It even pales the blood craving. I am *not* taking it off me." No matter what, that thing stayed with me.

"You're not alone anymore, damn it!" he spit. "You've got *me*!"

"It's not as easy as you think," I said, smiling at myself, shaking my head. If he only knew...

"I don't care if it's hard—let it be hard." He came in front of me and grabbed my ice-cold hands. "That thing will make a slave out of you eventually. How are you going to rely on it all your life? You've got me. I will help you."

"You can't! You don't fucking have magic!"

"We can do it without magic, too. We'll do whatever it takes. You can't rely on that thing forever. It will wear out. It's *magic*, and you're a vampire. You can't rely—"

"And what—I can rely *on you* for the rest of my life? C'mon, you can't be serious!" I spit...and I regretted it the next second.

Right when he looked like I'd slapped him across the face. He lowered his head just when I thought he would continue to yell at me.

Instead, he whispered: "I get it. I understand."

Shaking my head, I tried to reach for him, but he moved back. "Ax, I—"

"Hey, it's fine. I understand," he cut me off. "Let's just keep going."

And he disappeared inside the building too fast for me to try to stop him, leaving me alone again.

He *didn't* understand.

He just thought that I didn't trust him, which was *exactly* what I said, but I didn't fucking mean it. I had trusted him with Marie and Marcus, hadn't I? Right after I swore to protect them with my life.

And I'd trusted him with things I'd never told anybody in my life before. How could he not see that?

Fuck. We couldn't even make it to Arizona in time. Too many cities. Too many people. We couldn't run as much as we should have, but we made it close to Albuquerque. The sun had twenty minutes to rise, and we were both exhausted. I hadn't had blood again, but I'd had some pizza, which was fine. And we'd kept away from each other the whole way.

When we stopped near a motel, I didn't go in while he booked rooms. I wasn't surprised when he handed me a key. He could barely look at me, and I could barely look at him.

It was so fucking disappointing that, when I went to my room, I lay down without bothering with a shower or taking my clothes off. I didn't tease him or call him to me or even *want* him there with me, even if I needed him.

And he didn't make a single sound, either.

Eventually, the sun came out, and I was so desperate to escape, I fell asleep the same second.

When I woke up, I was in chains.

CHAPTER
FOURTEEN

My instincts screamed and my eyes popped open to find a chain around my ankles.

And somebody was trying to put one around my wrists, too.

I moved without really thinking. I pushed myself up from the bed and slammed my fists onto the bodies around me until they let me go. I rolled and fell off the bed, still completely disoriented, and when I tried to stand, the chains made it impossible.

I smelled the scent of vampire and magic even before I managed to wrap my hands around the thick chains. Somebody grabbed me by the hair and pulled my head up. I barely saw the blade of the knife as it came for my neck. The voices in my head screamed. I pushed myself back and brought up my knees with all my strength, catching him on the shoulder before he fell right over me, a fistful of my hair still in his fucking hands.

My fangs were already out so I bit the guy on his neck. Definitely vampire. He screamed, trying to get away from me, but I grabbed him by the hair, too, and pulled his head to the side while I tore through his flesh with my fangs.

He stopped moving, but another pair of hands already had me by the ankles and was dragging me. I pushed the body of the dead vampire off me and closed my hand around the knife he'd wanted to cut my neck with. And once he was off me, I didn't look. I just sat up and threw the knife forward, catching the guy who'd been dragging me right on the cheek. He fell back and slammed against the wall with a hiss. It hadn't gone deep enough to kill him.

And he wasn't the only one there.

Three more vampires were already running through the open door. In the time it took me to break the stupid chains from around my ankles, they were onto me.

They had knives and they swung them at me without hesitation. I moved until my back hit the bathroom door.

But by then, I was also wide awake.

I waited for the guy in the middle to swing his arm—he was slower than his friends—before I grabbed him by the wrist, twisted it until it broke, then took his knife from his limp fingers. Three seconds later, he fell to his knees, that knife buried in his eye, as dead as he could get. I jumped on his back to get to the other side of the room and run outside where there was more space to move, but one of them grabbed me by the jacket and pulled me back hard. The other buried his knife in my chest, missing my heart by a good inch.

Fuck, that hurt.

The voices in my head went mad. They fed off the pain in my body, and by the time I took the stupid knife from my chest and kicked the guy in the balls, I was already seeing double.

Not yet.

The other I'd stabbed in the cheek was onto me, too, his face a torn, bloody mess. I moved away as fast as I could, but they still cut through my skin and clothes. Not enough to slow me down, though.

When one of them slammed his fist on my chin, I let him. I fell back against the wall, and the moment he came closer to finish me off, I slammed my forehead on his nose. Blood exploded and he closed his eyes, giving me enough time to grab that knife from his hand. I stabbed him in the heart three times, then ducked down when the other two made to stab me in the back.

I came up with my knife ready, burying it in the forearm of one, while the other fisted me right in the eye. Growling, I stood still for a split second while he aimed at me again. As soon as his arm stretched, I grabbed it, then spun around with all my strength, slamming him onto the wall right next to the bed.

The wall broke. The vampire went all the way to the other side—right into Ax's room.

And Ax wasn't alone, either.

The vampire I'd stabbed in the forearm hissed as he took the knife out. I didn't wait—I jumped through the hole in the wall just in time to find Ax slamming his fists onto the vampire I'd thrown in there, until his skull broke. The guy didn't move again.

And the smell of magic had my stomach twisting even more.

Two sorcerers were in his room and another three were right outside the open door. More than that—another two vampires stepped into *my* room, too, as the guy with the bleeding forearm came closer to the hole in the wall, eyes on me.

I stepped back, and Ax stood up, too, hands bloody.

"What the fuck is this?" I asked breathlessly because there were sorcerers who'd turned their backs on vampires. Vampires I *knew*. They were from the Hidden Realm, and two of the ones I'd killed already were from the Redwood coven. Soldiers I'd sparred with.

"There's a bounty on your head," the vampire said from my room, slowly coming closer.

"There's a bounty on *your* head, too," the sorceress inside Ax's room said to him. Barely five feet separated us. Only walls behind us.

"We figured we'd team up and take you both out," the vampire continued, raising the knife with which I'd stabbed him.

I looked at Ax, confused for a second. Since when did vampires and sorcerers *team up*?

But Ax only grinned, wiping some blood from the corner of his lips. Had they hurt him? Probably—the room smelled like magic.

And I was already pissed.

"How about it, Damsel? You think you can take that thing off you? I could use a good show right now."

The fucking prick. "Sit back and relax, then. I'll give you one."

But when I moved, so did he. There was no time for talking or thinking or understanding. Those vampires were from the Hidden Realm which meant Jones knew they were here. Ax—I understood. He'd killed a lot of people while he was looking for me.

But what the fuck did *I* do to deserve a bounty on my head?

Never mind. It didn't even matter.

The sorcerers had already raised their hands toward us as they called for their magic. Colorful smoke in front of us, and the vampires were coming through the hole in the wall, too.

I grabbed the guy who'd told me all about the bounty by the head and meant to pull it off his shoulders, but he saw it coming, so he didn't try to back off. He pushed himself to the side and slipped from my hands, spinning on the floor, while Ax moved away to avoid the blasts of magic.

The other vampire came at me, fangs in full display, eyes dark and murderous. I was going to need those knives he was holding, so I didn't bother too much trying to kill him right away. I ducked down and spun with my leg outstretched to take his from under him, and when he jumped, I fisted him right in the groin.

Oh, that must have hurt like hell.

He was crouched over when his feet landed on the floor again, and my fist connected with his face immediately. I went for his knives, but I only managed to grab one before the other vampire came for me. He cut a clean line on my back, ruining my fucking jacket in the process, before I moved away and threw the knife at him. I caught him in the side of his neck because he moved too fast. It wouldn't kill him, but it would at least make him back off for a second.

I bit into the neck of the one in front of me, too impatient to get this over with already. Who cared *how* I killed—all that mattered was that they ended up dead.

And they did. I grabbed the knife from his hand, having to break his middle finger in the process while my fangs were still inside him and while he tried to bite my shoulder, too. But the knife was mine, and I stabbed him in the chest at least five times before I stopped biting him.

He fell to the floor with his eyes wide open.

The one I'd stabbed on the neck was coming for me. I waited with my back turned to give him a bit of confidence, and when he raised that knife to stab me in the back again, I kneeled and swung my arm back, the knife in my hand backward.

I stabbed him right in the balls.

He howled like a fucking wolf to the moon as he moved back, hands on his groin, not daring to even take the knife out of him as he fell against the wall.

"Really? In the fucking balls?"

I turned to Ax, his eyes sparkling with mischief even though he was covered in blood, too. And two of the sorcerers were already dead.

I shrugged. "I wasn't looking." He grinned widely. "Whatever. You probably liked it." He absolutely did.

But there was no time to dwell on that. I had to finish the vampire, and it wasn't even fun because he was so caught up trying to keep his balls from falling off that he didn't even try to stop me when I bit half his neck off.

Yuk. Vampire blood was worse than cow's blood, if you asked me.

Technically, *it was* cow's blood, if they fed back home, but still. It was much more disgusting.

"Need a hand?" I asked Ax as the blue smoke hit him in the chest and sent him sliding back until he hit the wall, too.

"Yeah, I could use a hand," he said, but he was having the time of his fucking life. I had yet to know a man who enjoyed fighting and killing as much as he did.

But I got to work, too.

There were three of them left, and they were all aiming toward us. They worked well together, too—they threw their magic at us one after the other, so that they had enough time to gather *more* by the time the other was done, leaving us no way to get to them.

Which was a bitch, because I had to intentionally step in front of dark purple magic smoke, just so it could hit me and knock me down—straight into the hole in the wall that would lead me to my room.

Fuck, it hurt. Magic was the worst, and it sent the voices in my head screaming again. To be fair, they weren't as loud as usual, but they were still there. I had to sacrifice half my focus on them, but the magic was already fading. I didn't give myself the chance to heal properly before I moved. There just wasn't enough time.

I ran out the door of my room, twice as slow as usual, and out in the hallway of the motel to catch the sorcerers from behind.

It worked.

The tallest of them turned to me, the yellow smoke in his hands growing by the second. I ran for him anyway. If he hit me, I was going down, but if I reached him, he'd go down with me.

The magic slipped from his hands just as I wrapped my arms around him. It was horrible. Like ice and fire pouring all over me for a second, and my legs gave. I fell to the floor with the sorcerer hugged to my chest. He tried to push me off with all his strength, and he was going to succeed. All that magic was no joke, and my limbs were so fucking heavy, but I was also a vampire. I had fangs.

So, I bit him right in the shoulder. He screamed much like the vampire I'd stabbed in the balls. He thrashed under me and tried to push his hips up. Eventually, I couldn't hold on any longer so I let go. I'd done enough damage to his shoulder and neck, and he wasn't going to be hard to put down now.

Except the moment he made it to his feet, his head

twisted to the side fast. He fell right back on the floor while Ax stood over me, breathing heavily.

"You okay?"

I smiled. "Just peachy."

He offered me his hand and I took it. I slammed onto his chest, holding onto his arm as the magic faded from my system slowly. The police were close, we could hear their sirens outside. And there were people in the rooms around us, though none of them had come out. Their blood was rushing, their hearts racing. They were terrified.

And when they came out of the rooms and saw the bloodbath we left behind, they'd be scarred for life.

"That was interesting," I whispered, looking at the bodies of the sorcerers and the vampires. *Together.*

"Can you run?"

"Move," I said, and together, we ran out the building like our tails were on fire.

We only made it as far as the highway before we heard the cars. We stopped running for a second, just to make sure we knew what was coming and which way to go. With all that panic inside me, and the whispers in my head, it was pretty difficult to do.

At first, I thought it was the police, but there were no sirens on those cars.

And the second I saw the color of the truck leading the way for another two, I knew.

I knew who it was, and my fangs came out again at the same second. The voices in my head screamed, too, but I was no longer even worried about them. As long as I had that pendant touching my skin, I was going to let myself be free of worry about them for once.

"Run," I told Ax, grabbing him by the arm.

But he was already laughing.

"It's him. It's Jacob Thorne," he said, and made to walk toward the middle of the street, right where the cars were coming. They would be on us before the minute was over.

"No," I said, stepping in front of him, so panicked my knees were shaking. "No—we run. They can't catch us."

"Fuck that," Ax said, his eyes bloodshot. "I'm going to kill him right here, right now." And he made to move again.

"*No!*" I shouted, pushing him back. "You're not going to kill anyone. You're going to run with me."

If I'd stabbed him through the heart, he'd have probably looked less surprised.

"He's right here. The night's young," he said through gritted teeth, looking at me like I was a three-headed alien.

"No, Ax," I said, taking his face in my hands. "I can't let you hurt him."

The way his face twisted, I thought he might collapse. Even his heart skipped a beat.

He shook his head, but he didn't have anything to say.

"I'm sorry," I said, tears pricking the back of my eyes. I knew I was hurting him. I knew he was jealous. I knew it all, but I would still not let him hurt Jacob. Because I also knew who that man was. He wasn't bad—on the contrary. I'd walked away from him, but that didn't mean he was my enemy.

"Please, just run with me. *Please.*"

The cars started slowing down. They were barely twenty feet away from us now. Humans were all out of the motel on the other side, watching. They'd probably seen the bodies we'd left behind, too.

Ax started to run down the highway without warning.

I turned around just as Jacob stopped his truck, eyes wide and lips parted as he watched me. *I'm sorry,* I wanted to say to him, too. So fucking sorry, I was sick of it. No matter what I did, I fucked up somehow. I just couldn't get anything right.

The passenger door opened, and Ray stepped out. Jacob stood perfectly still, waiting…

I turned and followed Ax down the highway.

CHAPTER
FIFTEEN

I couldn't keep going.

It had been two hours since we started running, and I was tired. I was exhausted. My limbs were so fucking heavy, and my thoughts were a chaotic mess. The whispers were easy to ignore now that I had that pendant. It was easy not to be terrified of them every waking second.

It would have been a relief had I been in any other situation, I suppose. And we were close to the Park now, but I couldn't keep going. I just needed to stop.

"Ax," I called, not really sure if he could even hear me. He'd run ahead and had never stopped to wait for me. He was much faster than me, apparently, so I hadn't been able to reach him, either.

But I was done running for tonight.

The town we were going through was big and lively compared to some. Jacob would never know which turns we took or where we stopped. At least I hoped not.

And if he did, I'd rather be somewhere where I could hear him coming. I'd rather have enough energy to run away in time again.

I looked at the street ahead, at the three humans outside, others in their houses, and I waited for a few minutes. Just stood there like an idiot and waited.

Ax didn't come.

With a sigh, I started walking ahead, so weak my limbs were shaking. But I wasn't weak physically. Yeah, I'd been hurt, and the stab in the chest from that vampire still hurt, but the wound was no longer bleeding. I'd most definitely survive physically. I just needed the rest, that's all.

But I didn't have the guts to go face to face with a human right now or the money to pay for a room if there even were rooms available in this town. So, I just kept going until I found the darkest, tallest building around, hid in the alley at its side, and climbed up the maroon bricks to the rooftop. It was quiet up there. The smell and the heartbeats couldn't reach me if I blocked them well enough. And that wasn't going to be an issue right now.

I sat at the corner of the deck, hugged my knees to my chest, closed my eyes, and I just breathed.

It was okay. Not the end of the world. Jones had sent those vampires after me. The *why* didn't matter. He wouldn't really need a good reason—that I was alive and I wasn't in the Hidden Realm serving him would probably be reason enough.

That sorcerers and vampires had somehow made a deal together just to get to us made it worse, but still not the end of the world. It had probably happened before, hadn't it?

And Jacob...shit, the look on his face. How *disappointed* he'd been as he watched me from his car. He'd trusted me, and I'd run away. He tried to teach me things I could never learn on my own, and I'd run away.

He was coming for me—I knew he would. He wouldn't

stop until he either caught me, or I did what I promised him I'd do.

Right now, it felt *impossible.* Nowhere to go. The whole fucking world had turned against me.

But even after everything, nothing hurt more than Ax. I felt his pain like it was mine. He wasn't *just* disappointed in me—I'd hurt him, too. He didn't understand. He didn't get it. And how could I even explain what I didn't fully understand myself?

I don't know how much time passed, but eventually, the tears I held back from spilling dried in my eyes.

And eventually, Ax found me.

I didn't move when I heard him climbing up the bricks of the building. I didn't raise my head when he jumped on the other side of the rooftop. His footsteps echoed in my head, and my heart beat faster. My body reacted to his presence all on its own, without my having to even think about it.

He stopped two feet away from me, the scent of him filling my nostrils before I finally looked up. He was still covered in blood, his clothes torn, same as mine. There was a black backpack in his hand, and he dropped it to the floor before he came to me. He didn't look angry anymore. He didn't look disappointed. He just looked...*sad.*

And it fucking killed me to pieces all over again.

He sat next to me on the deck, grabbed me and put me on his lap in one movement. I didn't dare move. He settled me on his chest, and I kept my eyes closed, afraid those traitorous tears would spill and ruin this for me even more. I just breathed in his scent, listened to his steady heartbeat as he held me tight.

All the thoughts in my head began to fade.

IT WASN'T SO BAD, was it? I'd overreacted. I'd been afraid. So what that those vampires had tried to kill me? So what that Jacob had already found me?

Did it really matter all that much?

Not right now, it didn't. It must have been an hour, if not more, and we still hid on that rooftop deck. I still sat on Ax's lap, and he still ran his hands all over my body, giving me back my strength and my calm with every single touch. I understood him best when he touched me, and I didn't mind at all that he was being gentle tonight. I think that's what I needed, even if sometimes I didn't know it. But he always did, as if he'd known me a lifetime. As if we hadn't met just a little over a month ago.

And somehow, it all made perfect sense.

When he touched the silver chain around my neck with his fingertips, I closed my eyes.

"Still jealous about it?" I whispered. Even though I didn't want to talk at all and just wanted to touch him, I knew there were things I needed to explain. Things he needed to understand with me.

"It was never about *it*," Ax said, pulling the pendant from under my ruined shirt. I'd even lost the bag full of new clothes he'd brought me, which was a shame.

"Then what was it about?"

Ax thought about it for a second, running his thumb over the silver buzzing with magic. "It was about you relying on someone or something else for anything, when I'm right here."

I gripped his shirt in my fists. "It's not like that," I whispered. "It doesn't just stop the whispers, Ax. It keeps the monster in control, too. The...the *spirit* inside me." Hiding my face under his chin, I forced myself to keep talking. "Jacob saved me that night. When they threw that house on me and set it on fire, he wrapped us up in a bubble of magic and kept us both safe from it. He said he needed my help to fight a greater evil that nobody even knew about. Said he could give me anything I wanted if I helped him first." I swallowed hard. "I agreed."

His heart beat steady. He absorbed my every word calmly, which was why I convinced myself to just keep going until I let it all out.

"He took me to a place where he trains other people. Five of them. They're all sorcerers. They all have Vein spirits inside them, too, and he taught them control. Taught them how to fight. He was trying to do the same to me. He would wrap me up in his magic so that I couldn't hurt anyone, and I would let the monster out and try to control it. I tried every single night, but I never could—until he brought me this." I touched his hand, still playing with the pendant. "For the first time that night, I had a little bit of control over the spirit. And tonight, when we were fighting, I didn't have to be as afraid as usual that it would break out of me and kill everything in its path. It *works*."

"What did you ask for?" Ax asked.

"To get it out of me. If I help him get rid of whatever monster he's afraid of, he will get the spirit out of me."

I felt it the second his breath caught. "Why would you want it out of you, Damsel?" he whispered. "This is who you are. It's who you've always been. It's a part of you now. You *need* it."

"I don't n—"

He pushed me back for a second so he could look at my face.

"You're *safer* with it. As long as you have that spirit, you're always safe."

"But nobody else around me is." The fear that gripped my chest was so intense, I had to grit my teeth to keep from shaking for a second. "*You're* not safe, either. Nobody's ever safe. I could lose control at any second, and when *it* comes out, it does whatever it wants. It kills. It doesn't care about *who* it kills—it just kills." As much as I hated it, it was the truth, one I'd never dared to speak out loud to anyone before. "I'm *never* safe with it, Ax."

"You are," he insisted, putting his hand on my cheek. "You're always safe with *me*, Damsel."

"No, you don't understand. I'm not, and *you're* not, either."

"We both are," he said. "Even if you lose control, you can trust me. Even if you attack me, you can trust me. I can take care of myself, you know that. You could never hurt me, Damsel. Not like *that*."

I shook my head, squeezing my eyes shut. The warmth of his hand on my face was the only thing keeping me from sobbing, and I hated how weak I felt.

He slammed me to his chest again, hugging me tightly. "You don't have to change a single hair on your head because you're perfect. You're *you,* vampire, Vein spirit and all. If you want to learn how to control it, you can. I'll help you. But you *never* have to change because you think you're not safe. You are. You're always safe with me," he repeated.

And I believed him.

I knew who he was. I knew he could handle himself. I knew he was smart enough to pick his battles. If there was one person in the world who could handle me *and* my monster, it was him.

And if it meant so much to him, I would do it. Screw

everything, the pendant included. I could be safe with him. It would be hard, but it would be worth it.

So, I grabbed the pendant and tried to take it off me, but...

He stopped me. "Keep it," he said, pressing the silver back to my chest. "But promise me one thing. The day you really trust me to take care of you, you'll take it off."

I wrapped my arm around his neck and whispered in his ear, "Deal."

"No more secrets," he whispered.

"No more acting like a dick." I could have sworn I saw him grinning, even though my eyes were closed.

"No more making deals with sorcerers behind my back."

"It wasn't behind your back, asshole. I thought you were already in the Realm!"

"And leave you behind?"

"I honestly didn't think I meant that much to you." Or I did—I just didn't want to admit it to myself because then I'd have had to admit what *he* meant to me, too, and I wasn't ready for that. I needed the distance. The time. It put things into perspective fairly quickly.

"You think I lied to you in the car?"

"No—I knew you meant it." When he said he'd burn the whole Realm to the ground, I believed him. He most definitely would. And as much as that scared me a little bit, it also made me feel like a fucking goddess. If that made me a shitty person, well...that list was already pretty long.

"I did," Ax said, kissing my head. "And when this is over, I'll have centuries to show you exactly what you mean to me."

His words combined with his voice set my insides on fire within a second.

I kissed his neck until my toes curled. "We don't have to wait until it's over. We can just start right now."

Suddenly, he pulled me up and spun me to him so that I was straddling him. My skin buzzed and my heartbeat tripled instantly. And he knew—that's why he smiled like that, like he'd already won. The cocky asshole. I kissed the grin right off him.

"Right now?" he asked while I bit his bottom lip, sucked it hard until he growled, then bit him again.

"Mhmm. Right now," I said, and his hands moved up my legs, right under my ruined skirt. I moaned into his mouth when he dug his fingers in my ass and slammed me to him. He was already hard, and when I rubbed against his cock, there was no more control left in me.

"Those fucking panties," he said as he ripped my panties in half.

I moaned. "We're gonna have to talk about you tearing my clothes all the damn time," I said, but I didn't give a shit about clothes. I just wanted to tease him.

"They're always in my way," he said, biting the side of my neck until I cried out. "I got you new ones, anyway. You're gonna wear them for me tonight so I can tear those off, too." His hand moved to my ass and his fingers slipped down to my entrance. My back arched as I moved against his cock, so ready for release it was ridiculous.

"Not so loud, Damsel," he breathed, sticking the tip of his finger inside me. "People will hear you."

"I don't give a shit," I said, rushing to unbutton his jeans, hands shaking until I grabbed his cock. I stroked him as he moaned even louder than me, thrusting his hips up, eyes closed, completely lost to the feeling.

Fuck, he was so perfect, even covered in blood like that, I wanted to eat him raw.

I bit his jaw, his cheek, his lips as I pulled up just for a second to position the tip of him to my entrance.

Then I sat on him and took him in all the way.

Fucking bliss. I could stay like that forever. The way he filled me was the most incredible thing I'd ever felt. He gripped my hips tightly and held me in place as he raised his up, going as deep inside me as he could. I cried out, so lost to the feeling I no longer saw or heard anything around me.

I started moving back and forth, slowly at first. He guided my hips, giving more strength to the thrusts, rising up to meet me every time. My clit pressed onto his pelvis with every movement. He stuck his hand under my shirt, under my bra, and squeezed my breast hard. My head fell back, and the orgasm took over me instantly, setting each one of my cells on fire.

Ax kept on moving for a while longer, making the feeling last until I couldn't feel my limbs at all. He *emptied* me and filled me up at the same time like nothing else ever could.

And when he came, he moaned loudly, giving my *mind* an orgasm, too. I loved the sound of him. He buried his face in my neck, wrapped his arms around me so tightly I thought he'd break my ribs for real.

While we were like that, I looked up at the open sky over me, the stars shining like they were winking at me, as if my pleasure had reached all the way to them and they'd felt it, too. There were really no limits to what this man could make me feel...

And then we heard the footsteps.

I jumped to my feet so fast, I'd have fallen right back down if I didn't have my instincts.

"Human," Ax said in a throaty whisper as he buttoned

up his pants.

The door of the rooftop deck opened, and a man stepped out. He must have been at least sixty—and he was properly pissed.

"What the fuck are you doing up here, you fucking degenerates?" he shouted at the top of his lungs, pointing a wooden cane at us.

I burst out laughing. "Jump!"

I jumped on the railing and straight down on the sidewalk in front of the building.

People saw. They stopped with their mouths open and watched me, and then Ax landed right next to me, laughing. The old man still called us names from the rooftop, looking down at us—the only one not surprised that we'd jumped four stories down and landed on our feet.

We started running down the street and we didn't look back.

CHAPTER
SIXTEEN

WE HAD TO RUN ALL THE WAY TO THE NEXT TOWN TO FIND A hotel. It was small and the room was smelly, but it had a door and a bed and a shower. That's all we really needed.

I still couldn't believe how relieved I'd felt to get all of that off my chest. It had been so hard to talk about it, and I constantly thought I would regret it or just feel worse after, but I didn't. I felt light as a feather.

Maybe it wasn't such a bad thing to tell people stuff, after all.

Right now, it didn't even matter.

As soon as we walked into the room and locked the door behind us, Ax grabbed me by the hand and took me to the bathroom. He made me stand there as he slowly took my clothes off, touching and kissing me as he went. Then he put me in the shower before he took his own clothes off, too, and joined me.

There was barely any space to fit the both of us, but we somehow made it work. The water was nice, lukewarm, and our hands were all over each other, lathering each other up. He was so deliciously hard that when I rubbed his cock, a moan ripped right from my throat.

"Keep going, baby," he whispered, while his hands moved down my chest and he rubbed my nipples with his thumbs. I was already burning.

"How do you want me?" I asked, and he squeezed my breasts hard.

"Every way imaginable," he growled. I pressed my chest to his, pressed his cock to my stomach and continued to run my hands up and down the length of him. My hips had already picked up the pace. I could imagine him inside me just fine until he actually penetrated me.

He grabbed my face in his hands and raised it up, then licked my lips slowly, grazed them with his teeth, sucked them inside his mouth gently until I was all out of breath. I was so desperate for him already, you'd think I'd *never* tasted him before in my life. I wrapped my arms around his neck, pulled him to me, and ran my tongue in his mouth until I knew every inch by memory. The sound of his moans and growls together with the water pouring out of the showerhead had my mind wiped clean of everything else. And when he grabbed me, spun me around and pressed me to the white tiles, I cried out in anticipation, back arched, so ready for him I could explode.

He took his time rubbing my clit with his fingers, teasing my entrance with the tip of his cock, making me beg like my whole life depended on the moment he'd be inside me.

"Ax, please," I said, pushing my ass back onto him. "Don't tease me."

"My greedy little slut," he whispered, and even before he finished speaking, he rose on his tiptoes and buried his cock all the way inside me. With one hand on my breast he held me in place, and with the other, he tortured my clit as he pounded into me, each time harder than the last.

I put my hand over his on my pussy to stop him. "Don't. I don't want to come yet." I wanted to enjoy this for as long as was possible.

He pressed his chest onto my back until I couldn't breathe anymore, growling in my ear. "But you feel so good when I please you."

I clenched my pussy around him, just like I knew he liked, and his fingers circled my clit even faster. He moved back and forth, in and out of me like he was in a race. There was no way I could hold back, no matter how much I wanted to. I came when he rose on his tiptoes again, his cock so deep inside me, I felt it *everywhere* on my body.

"So, so good," he muttered over and over again, thrusting inside me every second. I rode the high and clenched my pussy even harder, needing to feel him coming inside me. He felt incredible when I pleased him, too. I wanted to do it all day every day for the rest of my life.

And when we stopped moving, he rested his forehead on my shoulder, keeping his cock inside me still.

"We're not done yet," he said, like he really thought that we'd be doing *anything* else but this until sunrise.

"Not even close," I said, completely surrendered to him.

WE BARELY MADE it out the bathroom before he grabbed me again. Not that I had any complaints, but I hadn't even dried my hair properly yet.

He sat me down at the edge of the bed.

"Don't move," he ordered, then grabbed the backpack he'd thrown by the door when we walked in. He emptied it all on the bed—clothes, a small plastic bottle full of cow's blood, and a brand-new phone, too.

"What is this?"

"I stopped by the mall we passed on our way here," he said, then found when he was looking for in the pile of clothes—two tiny items made of dark purple satin and lace.

"When?" I whispered, as he lay the barely-there thong and the bra with the cups made completely out of beautiful almost-transparent lace on the bed.

"When you stopped on that rooftop first. I thought you needed some time, so I made use of it," he said.

"Wait—where do you even get all this money?" He just kept buying stuff, paying for rooms…I looked up at him. "You *stole* this, didn't you."

He grinned. "Nope. All paid for."

I squinted my eyes at him. "How?"

"I have money."

"How much money?" Because you'd need a good amount to spend the way he did for someone who was on the run from…*everyone,* really.

He scratched his cheek. "Somewhere in the eight digits."

My jaw touched the floor. "You're a *millionaire*?"

He grinned. "*We're* millionaires, baby." He brought the thong in front of me. "Feet up."

Shocked still, I did as he asked and he put it on me.

"You don't look like a millionaire."

He raised his brows. "What do millionaires look like?"

"I don't know. They wear suits, don't they?"

He flinched. "I don't do suits."

But now that I thought about it... "A tux would look good on you, though..." Those wide shoulders, and those narrow hips...

"Then you can get one for me when this is over," he said, then grabbed my hands and pulled me to my feet.

"Deal," I said, really looking forward to tear a tux off him.

Damn. Now I understood why he kept tearing my clothes off all the time.

He was so perfectly focused on putting those panties on me, it would have been funny if he wasn't naked and hard and if I wasn't already drooling for a taste of him. Screw a tux—nothing beat his birthday suit. I didn't even have any breath to spare to tease him about it while his hands were all over me like that. He grabbed the bra next. "Turn around," he said, his voice barely a whisper, that sexy whisper that my body adored. I turned around slowly, relishing in his grunts and growls as he put the bra on me. My nipples were completely visible through the lace.

When I faced him again, he looked so lost—cheeks flushed, eyes wide, lips parted. I ran my hands over the smooth satin fabric of the panties, then cupped my breasts through the lace.

"Like them?" I breathed, and his eyes lit up as he stepped back to see me better. Smiling ear to ear, I turned around slowly so he could see all of me.

But once I had my back to him, he was right behind me, his cock pressed to my ass.

"Fuck, Damsel. They're perfect," he growled in my ear, squeezing my hips. "Absolutely *perfect*...but now they need to come off."

I put my hands over his before he could move. "Don't!" I warned. "Don't you dare rip them. I like them!"

But all he had to do was press his cock against my ass harder and growl like a fucking animal, and my limbs shook. He hooked his fingers to the sides of the panties and pulled hard.

"I'll get you new ones," he said, and the fabric fell apart, biting into my skin, making me cry out.

"Fucking prick," I hissed, knowing I wouldn't be able to stop him if he wanted to tear off the bra, too.

Luckily, he didn't. He grabbed me by the back of my neck and pushed me forward instead. I put my hands on the bed for support, already burning with anticipation. The bra was forgotten when he took my legs and raised them up until I was on all fours. He ran his hands down my back furiously, like it was a race to see how much of me he could touch within a second. Then he squeezed my ass tightly and grabbed his cock, pressing the tip to my soaked folds, making my back arch all the way. I gripped the sheets tightly as he played with me agonizingly slowly. I held my breath, and my heart beat like a drum in my chest.

"Ax," I pleaded, pushing my ass back the second his tip was at my entrance. He moved away and slapped my ass hard, making me cry out.

"Don't be naughty, Damsel," he growled and took my hips in his hands. "Don't move."

"I won't if you do."

"You move, I stop," he threatened, and I cursed him under my breath a thousand ways. But when he brought his cock to my folds again, I didn't dare move a single inch. Damn him and his need for control.

And damn my own body for loving every second of it, too.

So, he played me with me for a little while, and I took from it everything I could. In fact, I was pretty sure I was going to come just by the feel of his cock on me, but he always loved to catch me by surprise. A second later, he thrust himself into me with a loud moan and my legs trembled. He had me by the hips, so I didn't fall on the bed.

Fuck, he was huge. I had yet to get used to the feel of him, and I honestly hoped I *never* did.

"Do you have any idea how you look?" he whispered as he pushed himself deeper inside me. "This fucking view, Damsel..." He sounded completely intoxicated.

"I want to see, too," I whispered. If we took this to the bathroom, he could do to me what he did two nights ago, and I would see all of it, too. I need to see his face, *my* face, our bodies moving together again. I was desperate for it now that I'd seen it once.

Ax stopped moving. I thought he was going to grab me in his arms and take me to the bathroom, when I remembered the sink here was *tiny* and it would never hold me up.

But Ax didn't grab me. Instead, he leaned to the side and reached for something on the bed...the new phone he'd bought.

I grabbed him by the wrist before he could straighten up. "What are you doing?"

"I'm showing you," he whispered.

And when he moved again, I didn't stop him.

Fuck, I wanted to see. I wanted to see so badly that all I did was grab the sheets again and squeeze my eyes shut when he started moving, thrusting into me slowly at first. He picked up the rhythm and my body responded just like always. When his hand circled around my hips and his fingers pressed to my clit, I no longer remembered my own name. The bed squeaked and moved, slamming against the wall, but that didn't stop Ax. He never held back from me. He took what he wanted, and I was a more than willing giver. For now.

Then it would be my turn, and I already couldn't wait.

I screamed out his name when I came, body shaking as the pleasure ripped me in half just like he did with my panties. He didn't slow down even when he felt me tightening around him, until I saw stars for real. He always knew what I needed, the prick. And he delivered it spectacularly, too.

When I came down again, he slowed his pace a little bit. His hand squeezed my ass as he slowly pulled himself out of me, then thrust inside me again with a loud growl.

Twenty seconds later, I was already on the verge of another orgasm.

"Move, baby," he whispered so slowly, I almost missed it from my own moans. And he stopped moving.

I got so excited, you'd think he'd handed me a million fucking dollars.

Taking it slow was fun and all, especially when I spun my hips around in a circle with his cock inside me, and he nearly lost it. The sounds he let out were better than a fucking award every time I discovered a new thing he liked.

But right now I needed fast. I needed desperate. I needed violent. So, I picked up the pace and slammed back onto him, taking him deeper inside me with every new thrust. I bit my tongue to keep from moaning because I wanted to hear him. Just his voice was more than enough.

"Damsel," he breathed, spreading his fingers wide and running that huge hand up the small of my back. Then he went down again and stuck the tip of his thumb in my asshole. Every muscle in my body locked as I came for the fourth time tonight.

He let go with me.

He bent over until his chest pressed to my back, wrapping his arms around me tightly. My limbs gave up, and we both fell on the bed, barely breathing.

Fuck, that was incredible.

And the night hadn't even started yet.

CHAPTER SEVENTEEN

"Where are you going?"

Lying in bed, I watched him put on his jeans, admiring his naked torso. Every scar on him, every curve and every muscle must have been made for my eyes because I could find no flaw on him no matter how hard I looked.

And I'd always believed that there was no such thing as *perfect*.

"Just to make sure we're still alone out here," he said, putting on his jacket before he came to the bed and pressed his lips to mine. The next second his hand closed around my breast, too, and he squeezed hard, making me laugh. Who was greedy now? At least the bra was still intact.

"You don't trust your ears?" I asked. We could hear it if someone was coming...wouldn't we?

Shit. I wanted him close to me so badly that I was willing to risk our safety for it. And that was wrong.

"Not anymore. I didn't hear the sorcerers at all last morning. They were probably wearing those damn shields. I didn't hear their hearts or their footsteps until they were right in front of the door," he said, but he wasn't worried.

He was grinning ear to ear as his eyes scrolled down the length of me spread out on the bed. His attention alone, the way he was so engrossed by me so suddenly, had my body on fire within a second.

"I can go, too, if you want," I offered.

"It's okay. I got it," he said and kissed me again. "Be right back."

He disappeared out the door. I barely had time to clean myself up and pick up the torn panties from the floor. Such a shame. They were so beautiful. Now I was really going to make him buy me new ones.

And he was going to tear those, too, probably.

I sighed, but I was smiling.

Before two minutes were over, I heard his footsteps and his heartbeat outside the door. It was incredible how I knew for sure that it was him just by the rhythm of his heart.

He walked in, jacket already halfway off, and he threw it to the floor.

"Anyth—" I tried to ask, but he moved lightning fast, wrapped his arms around me and threw us both on the bed. His hands were all over me in an instant. He licked my neck, too, right behind the earlobe, and it tickled like hell.

I laughed. Couldn't stop it if I tried. I laughed so hard there were tears in my eyes, and when he realized that I was ticklish, he just locked his arms around me tighter and kept going, not letting me move a single inch.

"*Stop!*" I shouted, already breathless, but he didn't. He kept torturing me with his tongue until I ran out of breath completely. Finally, he pushed back.

"Fucking asshole," I said, slamming my fists on his chest, but he only grinned. Fuck, I hadn't laughed like that in ages. It felt so strange, like I wasn't in my own body anymore as laughter still bubbled out of me.

And it was all his fault.

"I didn't know you were ticklish," he muttered, nudging my nose with his. "That's valuable information to have."

"Don't you dare," I warned, and I meant it. I wasn't a damn teenager to be laughing like that.

"I absolutely will," he said, not even fazed by how hard I was trying to keep a straight face. "I'll learn all your weak spots, Damsel. Then I'll explore them thoroughly."

"I will fight back," I promised him—and I would.

"Even better," he said, licking my lip.

"Don't be cruel, Savage," I whispered, eyes closed as he trailed kisses up my jaw.

"Haven't you heard? I torture people on the daily."

"By *tickling* them?" He moved on to my neck again, but this time he wasn't licking. He was kissing and nibbling on my skin instead, so I brought my hand to the back of his neck to keep him there. He felt so fucking good.

"No, that's only for you," he mumbled against my skin. "You have a wild laugh, too."

"Yeah?"

"Yeah. It fits you perfectly," he said, slowly lowering his hand down to my breast. "What more are you hiding from me, Damsel?"

"A lot of things," I whispered, as he continued to kiss my collarbone and shoulder. "It's gonna take a while to learn all of them." Lie—I was completely open to him. I couldn't hold anything back if I tried. He made me feel like *I* was getting to know myself, too, while he got to know me. Almost everything with him felt like a first.

And I knew how screwed up that was, how much

trouble I was in, but in those moments, I didn't want to even think about it.

"I don't mind," he said, slowly bringing his lips to mine again. "I'm a patient man. I'll uncover you little by little until I see all of you." He said it like it was the most wonderful thing he could imagine, like it was a future he craved more than anything in the world.

My smile faltered. "And what if you don't like what you find?" I whispered.

He leaned his head back for a second. "That's okay. I'll love it, anyway."

"How do you know?" Maybe he was full of shit. Maybe I was too much—and *I was* too much, always had been. Maybe when he saw it, he'd want to walk away.

"Because all of you, the good and the bad, is flawless. I love it even when you scare me. I love it when you piss me off," he said, pressing his lips to mine gently but not really kissing me. "And I love it when you fight me, baby."

I wrapped my arms around his neck and pulled him until he was on top of me. I liked it so much better when all of me was touching all of him.

"Then you're just as fucked up as I am," I whispered.

"I'm more fucked up than you know," he told me. "Just wait until you see all of me, too."

I grinned. "Aren't you afraid I won't like it?"

"Probably," he said. "But you'll love it anyway."

I hated how right he was.

"You think fate brought us here, Ax?" I wondered. Not that it mattered, but I'd gone twenty years without ever seeing him in the Realm, even from a distance. It made me curious to know why. Why *now*?

"No—Robert Sangria and Abraham Jones did," he said, trailing kisses up the bridge of my nose. "*We* brought ourselves here." I closed my eyes and he kissed both my lids, too. "I was going to kill you before I met you, you know."

My eyes snapped open. "What?"

"Yeah. When Robert told me about you, I planned to kill you before we reached the first town out of the Gates. I thought it would be easier. I only work alone."

"I only work alone, too, asshole. But I didn't plan to kill *you* without reason." And now I felt stupid for not expecting it.

He grinned. "Yes, well, I keep telling you that you're way too tame, Damsel," he said. "Besides, you did a damn good job stopping me."

"I did?" He continued to press his lips all over my face, and every new time, I was fuller.

No—I was *lighter*.

I was a little bit changed. A kiss had never had that much power over me before. Come to think of it, nothing ever really had.

"When you jumped into that waterfall, knowing I was out there, watching, I knew you weren't all that well in the head," he said. "I got curious. And when you saw me and you weren't even a little bit afraid, I was intrigued."

"Hmm," I breathed. "I am very intriguing."

He laughed. "You are, indeed."

"Did Robert tell you to kill me if things went wrong?"

"He didn't really need to," Ax said. "Did Jones tell you to kill me?"

"Yep." And I'd thought it would be a nice challenge, too. Boy, did I have no clue about what was waiting for me back then. "Have you seen him at all?"

He raised his head again. "Jones?" I nodded. "Yeah, I

saw him that morning. They were waiting for me in the Sangria castle when I arrived with the siblings."

My eyes closed. "Keep kissing me." He didn't hesitate. And when his lips were on me like that, it was just easier. Everything was easier. "What did he say?"

He kept his lips pressed to my cheek when he answered. "He looked me dead in the eye and asked me if I'd killed you."

Shit. I had no idea any of them had even thought I was dead, but I should have known.

"And?"

"I was hoping he'd pick a fight."

This time I pushed him off me. "It's Abraham Jones." He was one of the oldest, most powerful vampires alive.

"And I'm Savage Ax. Your point?"

Despite everything, I smiled as I shook my head. "You're hopeless."

"No, Damsel. I *was* hopeless because I thought you were dead."

He slammed his lips onto mine and kissed me furiously, knocking the breath right out of me. I felt his pain in the kiss, so much more clearly than he could tell me with words. I held him as tightly as I could to say that I understood. Just the thought of him dead that night when Jacob found him made me lose reason completely.

"How did you find out I hadn't?" I wondered. Who'd told him?

I felt it the second his muscles locked because he was lying right on top of me. He even hid his face under my chin.

I pushed him to the side and climbed on top of him so he'd have no choice but to look at me. His arms wrapped around me instantly, and he pressed me to his chest. I loved it, but I also wanted to know why he'd hesitated.

"Ax," I whispered. "Tell me how."

He smiled lazily. "Only if you keep kissing me."

I rolled my eyes just to tease him because I had no problem at all with kissing him. Pressing my lips to his, I whispered: "Talk."

And as I proceeded to kiss the rest of his face—and his cock proceeded to get harder—he finally spoke.

"A sorceress told me," he whispered. "The night I brought in the siblings, Robert and Jones wanted to take them. I made it clear that they weren't going anywhere without me, so they took me with. Apparently, what Robert called his *wine cellar* was just a cover-up for what he kept hidden deeper in that floor."

"Which was?" I said, pressing my lips to his closed lid.

"Alida Morgans, an old-as-dirt sorceress."

I stopped moving, sure I'd heard him wrong. "What?"

"I know. I was just as shocked to see her," he whispered, then brought his hand to the back of my head and brought my lips to his forehead again. "She's apparently a seer, and she's the one who told them about Marie. Robert said she'd *chosen* to be there and live in the Hidden Realm under the castle. She has a nice room with a kitchen and everything, and she's not chained or locked in any way. She reads books. She keeps the door locked with her own magic, too. She could get out without trouble every single day, yet she's still there."

"But...but how?" It didn't make any sense. Why would a sorcerer choose to live in a place made to separate vampires from her kind?

"Marie said she disappeared about twelve years ago, but she didn't know how. Everyone thought she was dead.

Her house had caught fire," Ax whispered as I kissed his temple. "Robert wouldn't tell me shit. He wouldn't tell me anything about Marie, either."

"Marie was touched," I said. "Jacob told me—it was a mistake to take her there, Ax. She really isn't a vampire."

"Oh, I know," Ax said.

"Why did they make us bring her there then?"

"I don't know. The sorceress knew but wouldn't tell me. I went to see her that day to ask her to make something to protect the siblings while I was gone."

My eyes squeezed shut and I kissed his lips hard. Thank the gods he'd thought of that. "Did she?"

"Yeah. She gave me these pieces of wood full of magic. Said to give them to the siblings and no other vampire would be able to stay close to them for too long. I left two of my people with them, too. They're staying in my house. So far, they're safe. Robert hasn't come for her yet."

I buried my face in his neck and squeezed him. "Thank you."

"Don't thank me, Damsel. I gave you my word," he said.

"What did she tell you?" I asked, not even sure what to expect.

Ax didn't say anything for a long moment. "Just that your heart was still beating."

"And you didn't doubt her?"

"Of course, I did. But I was going to kill all of them to pay for your life, anyway. If there was a small chance that you were actually still alive, it just gave me more motivation."

Every word of his rang true. I kissed him until my lips were numb. I tried to tell him with every touch how much he meant to me, and he understood. We both did. We both knew what we were. I knew he was a fucking psycho.

And I wouldn't have him any other way.

"Don't you worry about Marie or the kid," he told me, as if he could read my damn mind. "Soon, we'll be there, too. Then we can figure out what we want to do."

"I want them out of there. All three of them." The Hidden Realm is no place for a sorcerer. Marie and Marcus wouldn't be safe there forever, even with Ax's protection.

"Then we'll get them out."

He said it simply, like it would be as easy as going to pick up groceries.

"They're going to try to stop us." I was pretty sure he knew that.

"They will," he said. "They'll try."

"And what if we can't get them out?"

"There's no such thing, Damsel. You want something, you take it. It's as simple as that. Everything else is irrelevant."

I smiled. "That's not a very wise philosophy."

"It's kept me alive all this time," he said. "I always count on it."

Just like that, my mind was made up. I would count on it, too. Especially when it came to Marie and Marcus. It had been my job to protect them. I still felt like it was, and I knew what I was going to do—take them both to Jacob. I trusted him to know how to deal with Marie better than anybody else. He wouldn't hurt her—I knew that for a fact now.

But to get out of the Realm with them...I could never do it if I was only me. If the Vein spirit was no longer inside me.

That would truly be impossible.

"Why did he send those people after me?" I whispered

against his skin, not really expecting an answer. He gave me one anyway.

"He found out you're alive. The old sorceress could have told him, too. He wants you back. He knows what you are. *Everybody* would want you on their team." That was true—though not *me* specifically. Just what I could become.

"I trusted him." He practically raised me, or at least made sure I was alive since he found me.

"And he cares about you, Damsel," Ax said. "I saw it that night. He cares about you very much."

I sighed. "Why does this shit have to be so complicated?" It wasn't even fair.

"Let me go out there one more time, and I'll come make it very simple for you," he said, throwing me on the bed again before he kissed me.

"No—I'll go this time." It was only fair. And he was right—we needed to be aware of our surroundings at all times, especially now. Everybody was after us.

"Stay," he said, jumping off the bed. "I won't be long."

"I'm not made of fucking paper, you know," I said, a bit pissed but not at him.

Ax laughed. "I know you're not," he whispered, putting on his jacket again. "But baby, you're priceless. I'm gonna treat you as such."

"Yeah? So, what do priceless people do? Just lay back and...what—*not* even worry at all?" That sounded so...easy.

"Exactly," Ax said.

I rolled my eyes. "Fine, but you're spoiling me."

He opened the door, laughing. "Fuck, yeah. I'll spoil you every fucking day for the rest of my life."

And I was already a bit cold without him on the bed.

"Go!" I said, waving for him to get out already so he could come back sooner.

"By the way, you should call that girl. Brown hair, brown eyes. She was with Ivan when we went back." My stomach fell instantly. "She was pretty shook when I told her you died."

And he closed the door.

Anya.

I sat on the bed, looking at the phone at the edge of it like it was the devil. I didn't want to do this. I missed her so much it made me sick, but I didn't want to talk to her, not over the phone. What would I even say? How would I convince her to stop worrying, stop crying when I wasn't there with her? Because she would cry, I knew she would.

Did Jones tell her that I wasn't really dead?

Fuck, if I'd only known, I'd have forced Jacob to give me his phone—or even stolen it—just to tell her that I was okay.

But despite the fact that my skin was crawling, I picked up the phone. Despite not being able to fill my lungs with enough air, I typed her number. Hers and Ivan's were the only ones I knew by memory. And my old one.

My finger shook so bad when I made to press the Call button. I did it anyway. This wasn't about me. It was about Anya.

And the moment she picked up, I realized how utterly unprepared to hear her voice I'd been.

I froze. The words were there, at the tip of my tongue but I couldn't say them.

"Hello?" she asked, her voice low, barely a whisper. "Who's this? Hello?"

Get it together! I shouted at myself in my head.

It was now or never.

"Do not cry. Do not scream. Do not panic in any way, okay? Just get somewhere you can talk."

My voice was so dry and so strange to my own ears, for a moment I thought she might not recognize me at all.

A second of complete silence lasted an eternity.

Then… "Oh, hey. Mel. I'm with Ivan right now and I can't leave. What's up?"

My eyes closed and a loud breath left me. "I'm alive. I'm okay. I'm coming home soon," I said in a whisper, terrified that Ivan would be close enough to hear.

"Oh," Anya said, her fake cheerfulness evident even through the phone. "That's great, then."

My heart thundered in my chest. "Anya, I'm sorry," I breathed, then pressed the End Call button as fast as my fingers allowed.

Falling back on the bed, I closed my eyes and just focused on breathing. It was okay. She'd heard my voice. She knew I was okay. She knew I was going back. And when I did, I would explain everything to her. She'd understand. She'd give me a piece of her mind about it, but she'd understand.

Clutching the phone to my chest, I waited like that, half of me terrified that she'd call back.

She didn't.

And Ax finally came back.

"Hey," he said, not half as cheerful as he had been leaving. "What is it?" He took the jacket off and climbed on the bed next to me. "You watched it?"

I opened my eyes. "What?"

"The video?" he said, looking at the phone in my hands.

Heat rushed to my cheeks instantly. The video. Fuck, I'd forgotten all about the video.

"No, I called Anya," I said, then put the phone in his hands as if it suddenly disgusted me.

Did it? I'd had no problem with him recording when he was buried inside me.

Now, it just felt...strange.

"Okay," Ax said. "You okay?"

"I'm fine." I wasn't—and not just because of Anya. "Did you *really* record us fucking?"

His response was to grin and make himself comfortable next to me. "Wanna see?"

Did I?

Fuck, yeah, I wanted to see. But it was still strange.

I sighed. It was the perfect thing to get my mind off back home right now, but still...

"And we'll delete it right after." That was the smart thing to do, right?

"If that's what you want," Ax said without missing a beat and brought up the only item in the Gallery app. The video was paused, but you could see my back and my ass perfectly in the frame.

My cheeks burned. Holy shit, that was actually *me*.

"Don't tell me you've never watched porn before."

"Of course, I have. But I've never recorded myself doing it. It's different."

"If you want to delete it right now—"

"No, just play it for a second. Just...for a second." Then I could delete the video, break the phone, set it on fire, and bury the remains in the ground somewhere.

"Good girl," the asshole said, as if I wasn't heated enough by the idea of watching *us* having sex.

He pressed play.

The sound of his moans reached me first. The sound of our skin slapping against one another came next. The motel room slowly faded out of existence as Ax picked up the speed in the video, slamming his hips onto me as he growled and grunted. The way I screamed out his name was fascinating. The way the muscles on my back clenched every time I took him in all the way was mind-blowing. You couldn't see my face or his. You wouldn't know it was us at all, but I could have sworn I was right there again, standing on all fours while he pounded into me.

So fucking beautiful, Ax whispered. *You're killing me, baby. Your pussy is my fucking heaven.*

Words I'd *never* even heard while we'd been living that moment because I was too far gone and my ears were filled with my own moans. But this made the whole thing a thousand times better.

"Fuck," I breathed when I saw my own hands in the video gripping the sheets tightly and my back arching all the way as I came. So fucking sexy, I was having trouble believing it was me.

And then Ax slowed down his pace, and even though he'd moved the phone every time he'd slammed into me then, now his hand was steady. I remembered the feel of him slowly coming out of me, then going back in again, but the sight of it was something else entirely. His thick cock coated in my juices. My ass raw red from how hard he dug his fingers in my skin. The way I opened for him and the way he slid in and out of me so smoothly…

"What do you want to do, Damsel?" Ax whispered, his eyes stuck on the screen as he held up the phone with one hand, and with the other he rubbed his hard cock through his jeans.

I wanted to do that, too.

"I want to watch it again," I said, and a moan slipped from me at the sound of Ax when he came in the video, before he threw the phone away on the bed.

"Fuck, yeah," he said, pressing play again.

My eyes went from his hand that was slowly undoing his zipper to let out his cock and to the video of him slamming into me. My hand moved down to my lacy bra and I cupped my breasts. My legs spread to the sides all on their own. Fuck, I was so wet I was going to come in a second.

But I still tried to make it last. The video, and the sight of Ax jerking himself off, and my own fingers rubbing my clit, made for the biggest turn on I'd ever experienced in my life. I had to raise my hand every few seconds just to last a bit longer, and when I knew I was at my limits, I rose on shaking knees and straddled him. He put the phone on the pillow where I'd been laying, and we both looked at it and at each other. I took his cock and brought it to my pussy, teasing myself the way he liked to tease me.

The moment I sat on him and took him in all the way was the same moment I came in the video—and in the present. I exploded into a billion tiny pieces as Ax grabbed me by the hips and pushed himself up until he was as deep as he could go. I saw stars and suns and moons right behind my closed eyes, and I felt him coming even before the high let go of me.

The energy was sucked right out of me, and I fell limp on his chest. The video had ended, too.

The silence was only disrupted by the frantic sound of our heartbeats and heavy breathing.

"Still wanna delete it?" Ax whispered.

I smiled against his chest. "Let's keep it for a little while."

He slapped my ass. "Good girl."

CHAPTER
EIGHTEEN

THE UNEASE GNAWED AT ME. I HATED CARS WITH A PASSION.

"You sure we can't just pick up on foot from here?" We'd been driving a rental he'd had ready for us by the time I woke up tonight. He said we'd need it to get to the Park, even after what happened last time we were in a car together.

"Just a few more minutes, then we'll dump the car and run," Ax said. "Do you know exactly where we're going? The map says that place is pretty large."

"No idea. All I saw was the name." I should have tried to dig up more, and I would have, if not for all that magic that locked that house up.

"Do you know what we're looking for, though?"

I flinched again. "No clue. Just a *bigger evil* that scares Jacob. I think it's a Vein spirit—or even a touched."

"And you think we can handle it on our own?" he said.

"Not we—*me*." I didn't want him anywhere near whatever we were going to find.

"Sure thing. *You*. You think you can handle a Vein spirit?"

I shrugged. "You saw how that one in the alley ran from me."

"Yeah," Ax said with a nod. "I remember."

"Besides—if it's a person who's been touched, it's probably a sorcerer, and I know a bit more about them. I've been living with five of them for a month." And the reminder didn't make me feel good at all.

Jacob was something else. But the rest had been so fucking hostile toward me since day one, and that hadn't changed a single time. Not that I'd wanted it to—I was better off on my own.

Except with Ax.

"We'll be fine, Damsel," he told me. "Whatever it is, we can take it."

"*I* can take it," I reminded him again.

He grinned. "Sorry—*you* can take it."

I squinted my eyes at him for a second. "You're not going to stay away, are you." It was very obvious to see.

"Nope."

"Ax, c'mon."

"I will lie to you as many times as you need, but when it comes to it, I won't leave your side," he said.

"You f—"

"Think about it, Damsel. Just think about it. You know me better than to expect that."

I did.

That didn't mean I liked it.

But...I *loved* it.

Just like he said I would, the fucking prick. Ugh.

"How 'bout this, then: if you're in danger, and *I won't be*, which you know, you'll step back. Take a break. Regroup."

He raised a brow. "Okay."

"No-bullshit okay, or just okay?"

"No-bullshit okay."

Was he telling the truth? I guessed only time would tell.

But to be honest, I wasn't that worried. The monster in me was vicious. It was amazing how much power it truly had, and I could only tell now when I had better control of it and the voices in my head. It was amazing how much effort and focus and energy it had taken my whole life just to keep myself under wraps. And now that I didn't have to try so hard anymore, I felt reborn.

I couldn't wait to get rid of the stupid spirit for good, now more than ever.

The view took my breath away. The dark of the night enabled me to see everything in clear detail as I looked at the giant rocks in the distance, and the forested mountains behind them. The cold felt mighty fine against my bare skin.

"A lot of dams around here," Ax said, as he looked at the map on his phone. "A lot of mountain lions, too."

"They'll keep away." Animals had much sharper instincts than humans. They tended to keep away from us generally, though I'd never actually seen a mountain lion before.

"You think?" Ax said, looking at me. "I've always wanted to fight a lion."

I rolled my eyes. "You're *not* going to fight animals."

"Maybe there's bears here. I've always wanted to fight bears, too. I could probably strangle a grizzly without too much effort," he said, and I wasn't sure if he was teasing or not.

"There will be no fighting anything other than whatever is supposed to be here," I warned him, and he grinned.

"Sure, Damsel. Sure," he said, putting his phone away. "I don't smell any magic, though. Just fur. And snakes, too."

"Me, neither," I said with a sigh. "We'll pick it up when we're close."

"It might take a while to search this place," Ax said. "There are caves to spend the day in."

I flinched. "Let's hope it doesn't come to that." I was more than ready to see the end of this.

"Stay close, Damsel," he whispered, before he grabbed my face in his hands and kissed all the breath out of me.

Then, he started running.

Praying with all my heart that this didn't end in a disaster, I followed.

It must have been two hours before we heard the water. The river was close, and the forest pretty loud considering it was almost midnight. I saw owls and eagles, plenty of snakes, bobcats watching us from a distance as they hid behind the large trees. At first, it all looked the same to me while running, but the deeper into the forest we went, and with every new break we took, it felt like we were in a separate world altogether. No cars. No lights. No humans.

I drank the blood Ax got me and there was still a bit left in that bottle in the backpack he kept strapped to his back. We'd eaten steaks as soon as we woke up, too, and I had more than enough energy to fight whatever was coming, but I still felt uneasy because I didn't know what we would even find here. And if the night wasn't enough to search, we'd have to continue tomorrow, too.

"Come here," Ax said, taking off the backpack when he sat in front of a tree trunk. I went and sat on his lap like it was the most natural thing in the world to do. Much more comfortable than the ground.

"You're worried," he whispered when I straddled him, pushing my hair away from my face. "Stop worrying. We're gonna be just fine."

He meant every word. He believed it with all his heart. His face was open, his eyes bright and he even looked like he was *smiling,* even though he wasn't.

He looked *happy.*

And it made my insides twist.

I kissed him hard, wrapping my arms around his neck tightly. I wanted to be that happy with him so badly, but I couldn't. Not yet.

"I wish we were away." Somewhere where nothing could get to us. Somewhere where there were no vampires, no sorcerers, no spirits, no magic—just the two of us. How fucking pathetic, but it was true.

"I'm right where I want to be," Ax whispered against my lips.

"Don't you wish we wouldn't be running? That we could just...*stop*. And breathe." There would be no distractions. Nobody would be after our heads, and I would be free to do whatever I wanted without the fear of losing my mind and body to a monster.

"We've stopped," he said instead. "We're breathing. I couldn't fucking ask for more."

"You're pathetic," I teased, smiling.

"And you're already sorry for me," he said, wrapping his hands around my hips.

"So fucking sorry," I breathed, slamming my hips onto his. Just the feel of his hardening cock under those jeans had me shivering. Why couldn't I just do this all night, every night?

Growling, he slammed me to his chest and squeezed me until my ribs threatened to break. "Whatever it takes," he whispered in my ear. "I don't care if we're running or hiding or fighting—we'll still be us. Whatever it takes."

Squeezing my eyes shut, I kissed his neck. "Whatever it takes."

My jaw was already uncomfortable, but this time, I saw it coming. It happened every time he broke a little bit more of the walls I'd put all around me. For a moment, I imagined moving back, showing him my fangs, so that he would know.

For a moment, I imagined moving back, seeing *his* fangs, so that *I* would know, too.

But before I could even begin to gather the guts to move, something reached my ears.

Something that came from far away, a voice I'd heard before.

Every muscle in my body locked down tight, and my eyes opened. I didn't see anything in front of me because all of my being was focused on that sound I heard.

"Damsel?" Ax whispered, feeling how tense I was.

And...there it was again. A howling. A cry. A scream, all rolled into one.

I knew exactly where I'd heard it before, too. Memories took me back to that night in that alley, to the green shape of the spirit as it hovered in the air...

Jumping to my feet, I spun around slowly, looking at the darkness, at the trees, heart in my throat as I waited to see the glowing light of a spirit close to us.

There was nothing there.

"What is it? What did you hear?"

Ax was behind me, his back to mine, and we scanned the entire area together as far as our eyes could see.

"A spirit," I whispered. "I heard its call."

He didn't hesitate. "Which way?"

I closed my eyes and replayed the sound in my head. Then, I raised my hand and pointed west.

A second later, we were both running again.

The terrain was rugged, the ground rose and fell every few seconds. You never knew where your foot would land next. Animals stayed away from us. Eagles soared over our heads, and the more we ran, the better I heard. It wasn't just *one* sound I heard—there were at least three.

Which was how I knew that it was all in my head.

"Do you hear anything?" I called to Ax as we ran.

"Nothing yet," he said. Even further confirmation, but we kept on going anyway, running too fast for the naked eyes to see.

In the distance, two large mountains covered in green touched at the bottom. I was almost entirely sure that that's where the sound was coming from. It was going to take us a little while to get there, but I didn't plan to slow down.

"Over there," I told Ax, pointing at the mountains ahead.

The ground fell a couple of feet ahead, and we had to jump on air at the edge. The momentum took us farther than I anticipated, and I almost ended up slamming against a tree trunk with my face. Luckily, I moved to the side in time to avoid it, but it did slow me down somewhat. Ax was ahead of me, and I barely saw his silhouette as we ran through the trees to get to the other side.

It felt like days before the mountains were in front of us. They looked even bigger from so close up, and if it hadn't been for those haunting calls I heard coming from them, I'd have stopped to take a breath and enjoy the view.

As it was, we kept going until the voices became so loud, it felt like they were coming from everywhere, all at once.

And Ax finally heard them, too.

We stopped running, watching the mountains towering in front of us that looked so innocent to the eyes. Ax's fangs were out, too, though not for the reason I fantasized about. Slowly, he took the backpack off him and threw it to the ground.

"It's here," he said, almost as if he were surprised.

"Ax, I think there's three of them," I whispered, shaking my head at myself. *Three* Vein spirits? What the fuck could we do against that?

"We got this," Ax said. "Let's go closer." And he took my hand in his.

The warmth of him slipped right under my skin and warmed my bones in a good way. The panic and the fear was still there, but I was able to swallow hard while I held onto his fingers, and move forward.

We were going to be okay. We'd just look, see where the sounds were coming from, then we could step back and regroup if needed.

But with every new step we took, it felt like gravity itself was trying to stop me by pulling my limbs down. The voices in my head were no longer whispering, either—they were screaming. But the pressure to give up control wasn't there yet at least. That's how I convinced myself to just move, just see, because if I didn't, I'd never know what was out there.

The ground rose up a few feet right between the mountains. I expected to find a valley between them, something *normal*, with a couple spirits roaming around.

But then we reached the top and saw where the voices were coming from, and I could no longer breathe. My heart stood perfectly still, too, and my eyes refused to blink.

The screams in my head stopped abruptly, because they knew, too.

We were so screwed.

CHAPTER
NINETEEN

It was a steep slope, at least fifteen feet down. At the end of it, there was grass and there were bushes, and about half a mile farther, there was a lake with a large cave rising up in yellowish stone right in the middle of it.

I called it a *lake* for lack of a better term because that was no water. It was yellow and bubbles popped on its surface every few seconds, and it glowed a sickening yellow, too. The light of it made the stone of the cave rising in the middle of it look like the mouth of a monster coming to devour me whole.

And that was just the beginning.

The smell of magic was different here, too, just as spicy, but with something else mixed into it. Something like rotten eggs that came our way in waves every time one of those bubbles popped on the surface of the yellow liquid.

Floating over it, and all around it, were spirits.

Not three spirits—but more. Many, many more, and they were all that same yellowish green, transparent so that you couldn't tell where one ended and the other began. Too many of them. Way too many.

And they were all looking at us.

"Ax," I whispered with barely any voice, squeezing his hand with all the strength I had left.

"Fuck, Damsel," Ax said. "It's a fucking den of spirits."

Was *this* what Jacob had been afraid of? Because if so, then he was absolutely right. These spirits, they could ruin the entire fucking world if they left here. They could do it within a day, too, if not less.

And...*more* were coming out of that large cave. I barely saw them, as if they only gained light after they left the darkness of the cave and the glow of the bubbling liquid fell on them.

But these ones were different. There were fewer of them, and they were bigger. They floated closer to the rocky surface of the cave, too, as if they had substance and were heavier. Every hair in my body stood at attention as the spirits moved from one side to the other as if they were being rocked to sleep, their glowing yellow eyes staring right at me.

"Move back, slowly," Ax whispered, and for the first time since I knew him, he actually sounded afraid.

Good for him that his self-preservation instincts were working. Because mine must have broken to pieces.

I let go of his hand, not really sure what I was even planning to do here. All I knew was that this was *it*. This was why I made that oath. What I promised Jacob that I would get rid of. I only wished he'd told me there would be *spirits,* plural, so that I would have had time to better prepare for this.

"You have to step back, Ax," I said, chin raised as I looked at the spirits...right until they slowly started to come closer to me. Not all of them, just the ones who'd already been out of their cave when we got there. The bigger ones stayed right where they were as they watched me.

"Damsel, you can't fight them all alone," Ax said. "We need to move back."

"I can't," I said, shaking my head, and the howling spirits were coming closer. My gods, I had never seen a more terrifying view in my life. I was so afraid I felt like I wasn't in my own body at all.

But the fear made the spirit inside me come back to its senses, too. The whispers began, and for once, I was thankful for them. Thankful for the distraction.

"Of course, you can. We can leave. We don't even have to go back home—we'll disappear," Ax said, grabbing my hand again. His warmth did nothing to calm me this time.

"I can't, Ax," I repeated. "I can't walk away without killing them."

"You *can't* kill spirits!" he hissed. "C'mon, Damsel. Look at them!"

And I was. I was fucking looking at them. "I made an oath," I whispered, more to myself than him. "I have to try. I can't walk away from this." And it was safe to say I was *never* going to make another oath again without knowing exactly what I was promising.

Fuck, Jacob, I said in my mind. He could have warned me. He *should* have told me.

"Damsel, we can't win against them on our own," Ax said, and it was a pleading.

"You're not going anywhere," I said and let go of his hand again. "Move! Go back."

"No," he hissed. "Fuck that. If we leave, we leave together."

"For fuck's sake, you can't do shit against them!" Did

we really need to argue about this when there were potentially *a hundred* Vein spirits right there, coming closer to us?

"Neither can you," Ax said.

"Please, just let me try. If I can't do anything, I'll run back. I promise you."

"No, I wo—"

I stepped in front of him and grabbed his face in my hands. "*Trust* me. Okay? Just trust me. I will run back." And I meant it. If those spirits didn't move away from me, I would back off. I would plan. I wasn't going to fucking die here tonight. Neither of us was.

"Damn it, Damsel," he growled, bringing his forehead to mine.

"Just trust me," I whispered again.

He kissed me slowly. "I'll be right here."

I'd have preferred he moved farther back, but I could pick my battles. Right here was going to be enough.

"I'll be fine," I said, more for my own benefit. It was just Vein spirits. I had one living inside me, constantly screaming its guts out. If it came to it, I'd let it out so it could deal with those glowing things.

No need to be afraid. I had this.

So, taking in a deep breath, I turned to the spirits again. They were close enough to see them in much more detail now, which sucked.

"Damsel," Ax called, and I heard it. He was telling me to be careful.

I would.

Gritting my teeth, I jumped.

The magic in the hair almost scorched my skin. I didn't see it coming, couldn't even tell it was there. It was perfectly invisible to my other senses, but when it touched me while I moved right through it, I felt it. I felt it all the way to my soul.

For a long moment, I was suspended on air. The magic held me there, whatever invisible barrier I'd fell against, as if it was trying to decide whether to rip me apart or set me on fire.

It did neither.

The monster inside me roared. The magic let go of me and I fell on the ground face first, feeling like every inch of me was burning.

"*Damsel!*" Ax shouted from behind me, and his voice rang all the alarms in my head. I jumped to my feet, breathing heavily, limbs shaking, to see that I was right in front of those spirits now.

And none of them was making a single sound anymore. None of them was moving closer. They just hovered there in the air and watched me, different shapes, different eyes, different mouths on each of them.

A hiss and I turned back to look at Ax again, to see him trying to slam his fists on air.

Or on the magic barrier that apparently locked all around this place, and we hadn't even noticed.

But the magic wasn't letting him in.

"Stop it!" I called, so relieved I could cry. Now, even if he wanted to come down here, he wouldn't be able to. He was just a vampire. If it wasn't for the spirit inside of me, I'm pretty sure I wouldn't have been able to cross through, either.

Ax stopped slamming his fists on the magic. I faced the spirits, hands fisted and teeth gritted, determined to see this through.

I got this. I got this, I said to myself, but I could barely hear my own voice over that of the monster. Even so, I took a step forward.

No weapons on me other than my fangs. No plan whatsoever other than to move closer, see what they did, and let out my own monster to play.

The crowd of spirits in front of me didn't move an inch as they watched me.

I slowly raised my hand and grabbed the chain of the necklace Jacob had given me. It wasn't going to do me any favors now to maintain control. If I had any hopes of somehow killing these spirits, it would be through the monster, not me.

Another step forward, and I heard the hissing again. Ax was still trying to break through the magic. There was no time to even tell him to stop it again because as soon as I took the next step, the spirits started to move.

All of them started howling while they slowly pushed themselves back and to the sides.

My gods, they were moving away from me. They were moving back, and even Ax could see it, because he was no longer hissing. He called my name, but I couldn't turn. All I could do was watch the spirits moving to the sides, leaving way for me to walk all the way to the bubbling lake and the spirits on the other side of it, still at the mouth of the cave.

It gave me all the reassurance I needed. Letting go of the necklace, I started moving forward again, slowly, focusing on the spirits around me. But other than to cry that haunting sound, none of them came close to me.

It was *working*.

But the closer I got to the bubbling lake, the more intense the magic. I had to stop moving when I was ten feet away from it because I couldn't breathe. No air reached my lungs. Instead, the magic that went down my throat burned me like real fire.

And the spirits watching me from the cave rose higher over the ground. It looked to me like they were getting *bigger*, too.

Ax kept calling my name. I kept trying to draw in air and take the heat of the magic. If I could only get close to that lake, I could see more. I could make those other spirits move away from me, too.

And then...*what?*

I didn't know how to make spirits go back to where they came from. I didn't have magic spells. I had come here to fight a monster, for fuck's sake. Not a hundred spirits!

A mistake. That's what this was. As much as I hated it, I needed Jacob and his books and his magic here, too. That fucker was going to pay for setting me up with that oath, but it was already done now.

So, I took a step back, still struggling for air.

The next second, the ground shook. The surface of the glowing yellow liquid was suddenly full of bubbles, and when they burst, even more magic was released into the air.

The spirits began to cry out louder, and some of them were even coming closer to me, too.

I hissed at them, and the ground shook more violently. Keeping my balance was proving to be difficult, and that wasn't all. The bubbles kept on bursting, and more light came from the dark depths of the cave on their other side.

More spirits, just as big as the ones already at the mouth of the cave.

I turned around, ready to get the fuck out of there as fast as I could.

But just as I took the first step, the ground shook again.

I could hardly breathe so I lost my balance and fell on my knees.

The spirits were coming closer. Yellow light everywhere I looked. I had never been more scared in my life. Half my mind was made up to just take off the necklace and give up control. But I knew that monster well enough by now to know that it would *not* run.

It would try to stay right here and fight those things—fuck reason. And right now, I wasn't sure even the monster could survive all these spirits. In fact, I was sure of the exact opposite.

Ax screamed out my name, telling me to get up, run, go back to him.

And I tried again.

But the spirits were too close, and…something was pulling me back. My gods, I made it to my feet, and I tried to run, but something *sucked* me back, like the air itself was moving against me, trying to get me to that bubbling liquid, to those spirits, to that cave. And I knew for a fact that if I ended up in there, I was *never* coming out.

Using every bit of strength in my body, I pushed forward. I didn't turn to look—it was more than enough to see the spirits next to me, the same ones who'd run from me at first, now close enough to touch if I reached out my hand.

If I focused on them, the battle was already lost. Whatever was trying to pull me back was strong, but I looked up at Ax's face, focused all of my attention on him instead, and I moved. Whatever it took to get back to him. Even if the skin was pulled from my flesh, I'd get up there one way or the other.

The spirits howled. They didn't touch me, but the magic that pulled me back lost hold of me the farther away from that cave I got. And when I finally reached the edge of the valley, I risked a glance behind.

Nothing but shapes made out of yellow light, howling at me.

I jumped up.

I dug my fingers into the soil, barely any strength left in me. The spirits no longer just howled—they *screamed*, and it sounded like the roar of a dragon. Worse than the screams in my head. That pendant was saving my fucking life because no way could I make it out of here if I'd had to focus all my attention on keeping the monster in.

"Grab my hand!" Ax called from barely two feet over me. He couldn't reach out to me because of the magic locking this place up, but I could reach him.

The pull had my legs moving toward the cave, but I gritted my teeth and pushed myself up with everything I had.

My eyes were squeezed shut. My heart stood perfectly still.

"I got you."

Ax had both hands wrapped around mine. The light of the spirits howling right behind me pulled me hard.

Ax pulled harder.

Going through that magic a second time was torture, but it wasn't half as bad as what would have happened if I never made it through. My ears still rang. The magic was still coating my skin, dragging me down.

Strong arms were around me, holding me tight.

"I got you. I got you," Ax whispered, over and over again.

I believed him with my whole heart. He had me. That's why I let go.

CHAPTER
TWENTY

Hands on my face.

"Wake up."

My eyes opened but I still couldn't see anything in front of me.

"There you are."

Ax's voice slipped inside my dark mind. His lips pressed onto mine, and I realized I was breathing. Air was running down my throat, not spicy magic. I was definitely still alive, and my body wasn't even burning.

I sat up with a jolt and my ears started working again. So did my eyes.

We were somewhere dark, the only light coming from the outside, at least twenty feet away from us. White stone all around us, and it smelled like dirt and moss in here. A cave with a dead end at our back.

"Where are we?" I breathed, and my voice echoed. Ax took my face in his hands and forced me to look at him. His eyes were wide and bloodshot. He didn't look like he was smiling anymore, but he was there. He was okay.

"We're safe," he said, then: "Don't you dare do that to me again, Damsel."

"I had no idea that was going to happen."

Tears pricked the back of my eyes when I remembered. The way the magic had pulled me. All those spirits. The way that yellow liquid had been *boiling* right there in front of me....

He slammed me to his chest and wrapped his arms around me, kissing the top of my head. "It's okay," he whispered, but it sounded more like he was talking to himself. "We're alive. We made it. But you're never going close to that place again."

My eyes squeezed shut, and I pressed my forehead to his chest. "I have to."

"I don't care what oath you made, baby. I'm never letting you get close to that place again." He said it calmly, like it was an undeniable truth.

I pushed myself off him to look in his eyes. "Ax, it's not that simple." Oaths couldn't be broken. If I didn't do what I promised, I'd die.

"Then we'll make it simple," he said, pulling me on his lap. "We'll make it real simple. You'll constantly try to get there, and I'll stop you every fucking time." He grabbed my face and brought my lips to his, kissing me like he would die if he didn't. I felt his pain and his happiness rolled into one, but I still couldn't meet him halfway. Not like this. Not when I had this fucking thing inside me still.

It was the same as those yellow shapes! *That* thing was inside me...oh, gods. I felt sick to my stomach. I needed it out of me right this fucking second.

But how the fuck was I going to tell Ax that I had to go back to Jacob? That I was going to need him to come here with me to finish my part of the deal? Because that was the *only* way that Jacob would get the spirit out of me in return.

My gods, he'd been furious about a fucking necklace. He would *never* agree to my working with Jacob again.

And I would have no choice but to do it, anyway.

I could feel my own heart breaking. Even the sound of it was in my ears. Fuck, I didn't want to hurt him. I didn't want to see that look on his face again. Not ever.

"Ax," I whispered, knowing that I would have to tell him eventually, and I'd just rather get it over with right now.

"I thought I lost you again," he whispered against my lips.

"You didn't. But we need—" He didn't let me finish.

"Just give me a minute," he said, kissing me. "Just a minute."

I could give him all the minutes he needed.

My limbs still felt a bit numb from all that magic, and I had no idea what time it even was, how long until sunrise we had, but I moved anyway. I put my legs on either side of him and kissed him back, so desperate, so scared, I melted onto him completely. I wanted to have this every night. I wanted *him* with me every second. And I knew that if I went back to Jacob, he would lose his shit.

While we kissed, I tried to think up a way to make it all work out. A way not to hurt him—or myself. A way to get to the other side of this without too much damage. Because I was so damn tired of being damaged. I wanted to heal. I just wanted to be with him.

But the more urgent his touch became and the more he slammed my hips to his, the more the thoughts in my head faded. We were here now, and he needed a moment. I needed a moment, too, just to be glad that I was alive. We could talk in a bit. There was nobody around us, no heartbeat I heard, and no Vein spirits screaming anywhere in the distance.

So, I pulled the shirt off him, and moved up a bit when his hands reached for the panties under my skirt. He tore them again, and I loved the feel of it. I loved what it meant. Nothing had changed between us, at least not yet. We were exactly where we wanted to be.

Fucking in a cave in the dead of the night had never exactly been on my wish list, but here we were. I struggled with the zipper of his jeans until it moved and took his hard cock in my hand, stroking it lightly as he devoured my mouth with his tongue.

Suddenly, Ax moved, put me on my back on the cold ground, and fell onto me. My body was still weak, but I didn't mind. His hands roamed all over me, under my shirt and bra, digging in my hips the way I liked, biting and kissing my neck until I cried out.

I didn't even mind the way the stone bit into my back. All my focus was on his hands, on his mouth, on his cock, warm and pulsating against my wet folds. Ax was almost never gentle with me, but there was something to the roughness with which he kissed me and touched me right now that told me exactly how afraid he'd been. How much I meant to him. Fuck words—anybody could say the right words. But nobody could fake the way he devoured every inch of me. I relied on that completely for the first time in my life. I held onto him and let him convince himself that I was here, and I convinced myself that this was real.

When he positioned himself and thrust inside me, we were undeniably one. For real this time. Much closer than we'd ever been. I felt all of him, the blood in his veins, his pounding heart, each one of the emotions that ran through him. He fucked me hard, grunting and growling, whispering things in my ear I was too gone to even understand, but I didn't need to. I felt it all in the way we moved instead.

I knew the instinct would take over me even before my jaw got uncomfortable, my fangs wanting to slip out. I didn't think about it at all, I just focused on the pleasure of having him buried inside me, slamming against me every second, taking from me, and giving back so much more.

We held onto each other tightly, faces against each other's necks, and the pleasure climbed inside me just as fast as every other time. I dug my fingers into his back when he thrust inside me hard and stayed there, letting go.

I was right there with him.

The need to bite him pressed on my chest, but my body was still up there in the air somewhere, floating, even though I felt every inch of him against me. And when the waves of pleasure subsided, all that was left was the sound of our heavy breathing, and our hearts beating in perfect rhythm.

"Ax," I whispered, wanting to see his face, hoping against everything that I'd find him the way my entire being yearned.

I held my breath when he moved his head back slowly, as if he were afraid to look at me, too.

And when I saw his bloodshot eyes, and the fangs that had come out of his upper lip, my heart skipped a long beat.

He was right there with me, too.

When he saw my fangs, he suddenly looked awestruck. He pushed himself up, pulling me with him until we were both standing, looking at one another, too stunned for words still.

His fangs were right there. His mating instinct had awakened for me, too. My gods, what the hell was wrong with my heart? It felt like something was wrong because it beat different. Every beat was lighter and heavier at the same time. Tears welled in my eyes, too, but for the first time in my life, they were *happy* tears.

Here I thought I'd die without ever knowing what that's like.

I touched his curved fangs with the tip of my fingers and his eyes closed as he held me.

"Since when?" I whispered because I somehow knew that this wasn't the first time. That he'd kept it from me just like I'd kept it from him.

"The last night we were together, before I thought you died," he whispered, and it took all I had not to cry out.

"Me, too," I choked. That night, I'd gotten the urge to mate with him the first time, and it had freaked me out so bad, I'd run out of his room the next second.

He took my hand in his and held my fingers against his lips while he kissed them. "I was a fucking coward for not biting you," he whispered. "If I had, we'd have killed that fucker that same night." He brought his forehead to mine. "I don't want to be a coward anymore."

Despite the fear, I still smiled. "Are you sure?" I whispered. "Absolutely sure about it? Because there's no going back from this." He knew it just as well as I did, but I wanted to hear it. I needed to understand that he wanted it just as much as I did.

"Damsel," he breathed. "I don't want to go back. I never did. I was always right where I wanted to be. That's wherever you are." He cupped my face, kissing my lips gently. "Mate or not, I already belong to you, baby. And you're all mine, too."

He'd never said a truer thing.

"Bite me, asshole," I said chuckling, even though a tear

did sneak out of my eye. He grinned, and when he looked at me again, his eyes were more alive than I'd ever seen them before. He wasn't just happy—he was about to fucking burst, same as me.

"Only if you bite back," he whispered, and he wrapped his arms around me, bringing my face right to his neck, and his to mine. My fangs were ready, and so were his. When he grazed my skin with them, I squeezed my eyes shut, the pleasure that went through me completely senseless. I'd been bitten by vampires before. It wasn't a sexy experience.

But no general rule ever applied when it came to Ax.

"See you on the other side," I whispered and opened my mouth. I'd never been more ready in my life.

And...

"*Stop.*"

It felt like the voice came from a dream. I remember trying to move, but Ax didn't let me. He pulled me back to his chest again.

Could he hear that voice, too?

Did he know who it belonged to?

Because I did.

"Stop it, Nicole," Jacob said, and the smell of magic barely reached my nostrils. My fangs were pressed to Ax's skin, and every instinct in my body wanted me to *bite* already.

But...

"If you bite him, he dies."

The entire world stopped moving for me.

Ax dug his fingers into my back. His fangs were ready, too. I felt them on my skin. He was ready. He was waiting. He would meet me halfway.

"There's too much magic in you, Nikki," Jacob continued, and I still heard him like the voice was coming from a dream. "It will kill him on the spot. He won't be able to survive it."

My eyes closed. My instincts reacted instantly. The voices in my head whispered, but I no longer heard them. All I heard was Jacob.

My fangs retreated before I even realized it.

"Damsel, no," Ax whispered, holding me tight to his chest, not wanting to let go.

And I didn't want to let go, either.

I did it anyway.

"I'm sorry," I choked, so full of hate for what I was so suddenly, it would have brought me to my knees if he wasn't holding me up.

"Look at me, baby," he whispered, slowly pulling his head back. "He's a liar. We were made for this. You know it."

His eyes no longer looked alive. "What if he isn't?"

And Jacob went at it again: "He'll die, Nikki. He's a vampire. He won't make it."

Ax growled, eyes gleaming, but he didn't look back to where Jacob's voice was coming from. And now that I was no longer lost in the spell of the mating instinct, I could hear his heartbeat. I could hear all six of their hearts beating just at the entrance of the cave, twenty feet away from us.

"Damsel, please," he whispered to me, and he served me his whole soul in that pleading. Mine to take. Mine to break.

It wasn't even an option. It wasn't about me believing him or believing Jacob.

If there was just a small chance that I could kill Ax with my own hands, that I could hurt him in any way, I wouldn't do it. Fuck everything else—I wouldn't do it.

It was as simple as that.

"I'm sorry, Ax," I whispered again because it was clear to me that this is as far as we went for now.

"No," he said. "I won't let you."

But I already knew he would. "I have to go with them. I have to finish this first," I tried, knowing he wouldn't understand me.

"You don't have to do anything you don't want to do," he said instead.

"I made an oath. I gave my word. It's the only way I'll be free," I told him, and the tears that slipped down my cheeks now were the saddest I'd ever cried. I could see how much I was hurting him, and I had to keep going.

"You're already free," Ax said, but his words were angry, too. Because he knew as well as I did that I wasn't going to run with him again. I couldn't. It hurt, but it was the only way I could have a fucking life with him in the first place.

"I'm not," I told him. "But I will be. And I'll find you."

I kissed him, but he didn't kiss me back. That was okay.

"Don't kill people for me, okay? I will find you, Ax. I swear on everything I have, I'll find you when this is over."

"Don't do this, Damsel," he said. "You don't have to. We're stronger together. He's lying. We're vampires."

"I can't risk it." If there was the smallest chance, I wouldn't.

He dug his fingers on my back so hard, it hurt. "You don't have to do this," he pleaded.

And I knew that the longer I stayed here, the worse it was going to get.

My gods, moving away from him was a different kind of torture. Just when I thought I'd felt all the pain I was going to feel, something happened to show me a whole new level of it.

"I know," I forced myself to say. "I want to."

It was like I'd ripped his heart right out of his chest.

Ax looked defeated. He looked like he'd given up. He let go of me, watching me like I was worse than those spirits in that cave.

Right now, I was.

"Think about it. You're *choosing* this," he told me, and it was a warning.

My own heart almost beat right out of my chest. "I am."

Ax didn't say anything else. He never looked away from me while I backed off, surprised to be standing with every new step I took. And I didn't look away from him.

Jacob and the others were right behind me now.

"Nikki," he said, but I didn't want to fucking hear it.

"*Don't* talk to me," I spit. "Get out."

"I can't—"

"Get out, Jacob. Right now."

I knew what he wanted—Ax. He was hired to find him that night. He was going to kill him that night, too, before I stopped him. And if he thought I was going to let him do it now, he was in for the surprise of his life.

"This isn't over," Jacob whispered, and he was talking to Ax. Whether he heard him or not, I had no idea. His face was perfectly expressionless as he looked at me.

And Jacob and his friends finally moved out of the cave, slowly.

I tried to follow, but it felt like my soul was being ripped right out of my body. My mind came up with a thousand reasons why I didn't have to do this. We could run. We could escape. We could make sure nobody ever found us. We could take care of ourselves.

Except...I'd made that oath.

And even if I hadn't, I wasn't free to be with him the way he deserved. The way I wanted.

There was a reason why I made that deal with Jacob. There was a reason why I stayed with him for a whole fucking month, even though all I did was fail. There was a reason why I agreed to however long it took just to be free.

"I'll find you," I promised him again. Barely any voice left me, but he heard.

"Don't bother," he said, and he sounded like he was disgusted with me.

My knees shook harder. Ax looked away, moving to grab his shirt and jacket from the ground. He turned his back to me, too, while he put them on.

His heart no longer pounded. His blood no longer rushed.

He was done.

It took all I had not to run back to him. It took everything just to turn around and step out of that cave. I was leaving everything behind me. *Everything*—but I walked ahead, anyway.

The scent of magic led east, but I didn't follow it right away. Wherever Jacob and his people were, I would find them. I just needed a second first.

When I was close enough to a tree trunk, I let go of my body and fell on the ground. I focused on breathing, on calming down my heart. I focused on *why* I was walking away. I gave myself all the reasons again and again, but none of it made it any easier.

He would understand. When this was over, Ax would understand. He didn't mean what he said—he'd understand. And I'd say that to myself as many times as I needed until I believed it.

"Nicole."

I looked ahead to find Jacob standing alone among the trees, about thirty feet away from me. The sky was beginning to turn grey with new light. And I had to keep going.

It helped to know Jacob was watching me. It helped in making me gather some strength to stand up. The cave was right there to my side, but I didn't dare look at it. If Ax was standing there, watching, I was afraid I'd cave. So, with my eyes ahead, I walked like I was a stranger in my own body, until I was right in front of Jacob.

I gripped his jacket tightly, even though my fists shook. "If you lied to me—"

But he didn't let me finish. "I didn't." Grabbing my wrists, he pushed my hands off him. "He would never survive. The spirit would kill him on the spot."

"So why did you stop me?" I whispered. He was hired to kill Ax, wasn't he? Why stop me if he knew it would kill him? *Please, tell me it isn't true.*

Jacob shook his head. "Because I still need you here, Nikki. I need *all* of you. I think you already know why."

With that, he turned around and started walking back to wherever he came from.

He still needed me here. And I still needed that fucking spirit out of me. If I'd have killed Ax, I would be dead, too. Not physically, only where it mattered most.

I couldn't have that, not now. So, I followed Jacob, holding onto the tree trunks as I went.

And I didn't look back.

CHAPTER
TWENTY-ONE

My eyes felt like they were bleeding. We were already in Minnesota. A fucking trap, just like the ones I'd been living in my whole life. The homes Jones sent me to as a kid. The Hidden Realm. This fucking house full of sorcerers.

My own damn skin.

All of them traps.

But they'd never felt quite so terrible before.

Because I never knew life could be better. I never knew I'd *want* to live so badly. I always thought I was okay with dying. I'd never *truly* wanted to be alive, not the way most people did.

Half of me hated his guts for it. I had been just fine living in ignorance. Not knowing had perks. I'd accepted that that was all there was to life, and I never had to wonder again.

But the other half of me was so thankful to him for showing me. So fucking grateful for the purpose he gave me. And the guilt of knowing how badly I'd hurt him suffocated me worse than the heat of the sun.

When Jacob stopped his truck at the back of the house,

the others were right behind us. I stayed there in the passenger seat, the sun at my back, my eyelids so heavy I barely held them open. I wanted to wait for them to get inside first so that I wouldn't have a reason to lose it. I would not be able to keep control in this condition if they provoked me.

But when the others disappeared behind the house, none of them even looking my way, Jacob didn't let me get out of the car still.

"Do you love him?"

His voice was barely a whisper, the words light as air.

Did I love Ax? No, what I felt for him was much more than love. I lived for him.

I kept my eyes on the wall of the back of the house. "You tricked me."

Jacob sighed, pressing his forehead to the steering wheel for a second. "If I'd have told you all of it, you'd have never agreed."

Laughter bubbled out of me and I fell back on the seat, too tired to hold myself upright. "And here I thought you were the good guy." Sometimes, I even surprised myself with how naive I could be.

"I *am*," Jacob insisted.

"No, Jacob. You just have a good-guy complex, that's all. You're just as rotten on the inside as the rest of us." The words flowed easy. I didn't even have to think about them at all.

He gripped the steering wheel so tightly, his knuckles turned white.

"I am trying to save the fucking world here," he said through gritted teeth.

At that, I had to turn to him. "*How?*" I demanded. "By tricking people who are hopeless into making fucking blood oaths with you so you can take advantage of them?! Is that how you save the fucking world?"

Suddenly both his hands were on my face and he was so close to me, all I could see were his bloodshot eyes. It took all I had not to jump him or slam my forehead on his nose.

"The last thing *you* are is hopeless, Nikki Arella," he spit. "You have the power, and you have the responsibility. Look me in the eye and fucking tell me you'd have agreed to help if you couldn't get something out of it for yourself."

"Exactly," I said. "But I'm not ashamed of that. I always knew what I was. And now I know what *you* are, too." I went even closer to him until the tips of our noses touched, just in case he thought he scared me. "This doesn't make you a *good guy,* Jacob. This makes you an opportunist. Look *me* in the eye and tell me you wouldn't have killed me that night if I hadn't agreed to help you."

His eyes widened, just like I thought. "You were killing our—"

"No—*you* ambushed us. *You* attacked us! I was there, dipshit," I hissed and pushed his hands off me. He fell back against the driver's door, the anger disappearing from his face. Now, he just looked disappointed. In me...or himself? I didn't really care.

"Don't lecture me about power and responsibility. I didn't fucking choose this spirit, Jacob. And you are *not* God." I opened the door and walked out in the scorching sun, knees still shaking. But the anger helped in pushing me forward, until...

"You won't make it."

I stopped in my tracks, thankful that I was close enough to the house to hold onto the wall.

Jacob slammed the truck door shut and slowly came to

me. I didn't have the strength to turn or the patience to look at him.

"I've spoken to some people. Found some scripts from my great-great grandfather," he whispered. "If I separate you from your spirit, there's a ninety percent chance you'll die. That spirit is the only thing keeping you alive since you turned into a vampire." My eyes squeezed shut and my legs shook harder. "Without it, the residue of its magic is going to turn against the vampire virus in your body and kill it, too."

I hit the ground on my knees before I realized it. My body was barely functioning.

And Jacob had the decency to put his hand on my shoulder.

"Nikki, I'm sorry," he whispered.

"Don't fucking touch me." I had no strength to push him off, but by the gods, I'd let out every monster in the world just to cut that fucking hand off in a second if he didn't move it away.

He did.

"I'm sorry," he said, and with his head down, he walked away to the other side of the house, leaving me alone.

I fell on the ground on my ass and rested my back to the wall for a second. The blue of the sky looked beautiful, even more so because the sun that made it so beautiful hurt me. It was a different pain, one that felt *easy* now that my mind was threatening to explode and my body refused to move.

And I thought I had it all figured out.

My shoulders shook with laughter even though barely any sound left me. Tears wet my cheeks, but I hardly felt them. I laughed and cried like a lunatic, looking at the sky, breaking to pieces every second.

"Is that all you got?" I asked whatever god could hear

me. Was that everything they were going to throw in my way? Did they think they were going to stop me?

I raised my middle fingers to the sky.

And I still didn't get an answer.

My eyes opened with nightfall. My body was still weaker than it had ever been before at this time of day.

I stood up from the bed, anyway.

All my instincts screamed at me to get back under the blanket, close my eyes, and just ignore the world for as long as it took.

I got dressed anyway.

My reflection in the mirror showed me just how much I was ready to give it all up right now and let go.

I went in the shower and came out clean anyway.

And even though I could hear the voices of the other touched sorcerers inside the house, I walked out, anyway.

As soon as they heard the door closing, they stopped talking. They were all sitting in the living room, watching some show, talking. But they all held their breaths while I walked down the narrow hallway. All their eyes were on me when I made it to the front door. I didn't turn to them. I didn't say anything. I just walked out of the house.

Jacob's heart beat like a drum in my ears. He wasn't close, but I could still hear him.

"You were right."

His words reached my ears slowly. My eyes squeezed shut, and despite my better judgment, I started walking again. He was sitting on the rocks near the spring, reaching out his hand so the water could touch his fingers, just like I always did. It calmed me sometimes. Maybe it calmed him, too.

I didn't cringe at the sight of him. I didn't hate him with all my being like I had earlier when we first came here. Part of me understood him. The other part...it didn't care because everything was already done.

"I know," I said, leaning against the rocks on the other side of the spring. "But which part in particular are you talking about?"

He chuckled. "All of it, I think. I tricked you. I used you because I knew you had no other options. I made you a promise that will probably end with you dead." He raised his head and met my eyes. "I'm no good guy, apparently."

"Welcome to the real world," I said. There was no such thing as *good* guys in the real world.

"I'm sorry, Nikki," he said, looking down at the water of the spring again.

"Don't be. I would have done the same thing."

"But you never claimed to be good."

"I was never a fan of lying to myself."

Jacob nodded. "I'm going to release you from your oath. And you're going to release me from mine."

Now that was definitely a surprise. I raised my brows. "Is that so?"

He looked at me again. "Yes. I should have told you the truth from the beginning. And I should have learned more about you before giving you my word that I could help you. This arrangement was not made on honest terms. You can't really force anyone to help you when they don't want to. I understand that now."

I grinned. "Wow, you're such a good guy, Jacob. I'm in fucking awe."

He smiled, too, shaking his head. "I really am sorry." And I heard it in his voice, too.

The problem was, *sorry* wasn't going to change shit.

"How about you tell me what you should have told me before I made that oath?" I turned and jumped on the rocks to sit down. My legs were still weak. My entire body, actually.

"You already saw," Jacob said with a flinch.

"I did, but I have no clue what the fuck that was." Just spirits and bubbling yellow liquid and caves.

"You sure you want to know?" He actually sounded surprised.

"Yes, Jacob. I want to know."

"It's a Vein," he said the next second. "A Ley line that broke the surface of the earth, something that was most definitely not supposed to happen."

"A Vein?" I said, shaking my head. "Aren't those supposed to be invisible and rooted deep underground, close to the planet's core?"

"They were supposed to be far away from the surface, yes. And we thought they were invisible, too. But you saw it. It's right there."

I shook my head. "It looked like a contaminated lake or something."

"Yeah—contaminated with magic. Do you have any idea how much magic is in that area?" he said. "It's more than two hundred powerful sorcerers combined. It's literally like a physical portal to the Ley lines. Spirits can come and go as they please."

"Oh, I felt it. I was in there," I said with a flinch. I remembered perfectly what it was like to be there, to not be able to breathe. I remember the magic, too, and the way it had sucked me in.

"Really," Jacob whispered. "You were inside the ward?"

"Yep. I went through. It felt like it *wanted* to stop me, but it didn't. Ax couldn't break through." I remembered how he'd slammed his fists on the invisible magic, too. His desperation. The pain in his eyes. His rage...

My stomach turned and twisted so hard, I thought I might throw up.

"And? How did you get out?" Jacob said, jumping off the rocks to come closer to me.

"The first spirits around the bubbling lake stayed away from me," I started.

"Yes, those are generally the weakest, able to get farther away from the lines," Jacob said.

"Yeah. There were others inside the cave. Those were bigger, and they felt more powerful. I thought they might stay away, too. Thought maybe they were protecting some big monster in that cave, but no. And even more were coming out before the cave or the lake or even *they* started to pull me back."

Jacob flinched. "You shouldn't have done that."

"I wouldn't have if you'd have told me what the fuck was happening there," I reminded him. He swallowed hard. "Anyway, Ax was right behind the ward, and I managed to grab his hand. He pulled me out." And then I left him.

Just like that.

Jacob sighed, lowering his head. "It didn't kill you." Then he laughed bitterly. "Nobody's ever been inside that ward before, Nikki."

I flinched. "Thanks for telling me that, asshole."

"I can't get through, either. I'd have to break the ward, and right now, that thing's the only reason why those spirits aren't loose in the world."

"Who made the ward?"

"Nobody. It's the Ley lines themselves, I think. It was there when the site was first found."

I narrowed my brows. "Wait—why not just go over there and send them all back? That's what you do, isn't it?" Sorcerers knew how to handle Vein spirits perfectly.

"We've tried, except the Vein is right there. They just come right back out that cave, which I'm pretty sure is their access to the Ley lines underground," Jacob said.

"Well, shit." That didn't sound good at all. "So why did you even bring me here? And the others?" It sounded to me like a lost cause already.

"Because we need to close that cave. We need to ruin it, put magic on it so it can't break through, something even stronger than that ward keeping them locked to that place for now," Jacob said.

Chills rushed down my back "What do you mean, *for now*?"

"I mean that ward isn't going to hold them there forever. Eventually, it will break, and when it does, every spirit of the Ley lines will have free access to the world, and if we send them back, they'll just return within the day."

"Are you serious?" He'd actually meant it when he said he was trying to *save the world*?

"Unfortunately, I am," Jacob said. "Which is why it was important to gather all of you here."

"But what you're saying is that it's impossible." That's what it sounded like to me.

"No—just really hard. I have a plan. I will see it through. But I can't do it on my own. I need people who have been touched, who are strong enough to get close to the Ley line itself without dying. I need them to ruin that cave before I can break down the ward and make another one around it—and that's just the first step. Then, I'd have to figure out a way to make sure the Ley line never makes it back to the surface again, too." He smiled bitterly. "And I have no fucking clue how I'm gonna do that."

Damn. Now I felt a bit guilty for saying all those things to him.

"What happens if you fail?" I asked, but I already knew. He didn't have to tell me. Vampires spoke about Vein spirits all the time in the Hidden Realm. It's the one thing that terrified them so much more than sorcerers.

Jacob shrugged and his heart skipped a long beat. "Then we all die." As simple as that.

And *all* meant Ax, too. And Anya. Even Jones.

All.

"Anyway, I won't let it get to that. I'll figure it out. There's time," he said, nodding. "That's not your problem anymore. We'll have to do the ritual again to release ourselves from our deal. I can't do it on my own without you agreeing to it. And then...you're free."

I smiled. "I'll just be free to go." Not *free* the way I needed to be. "I'm staying, Jacob. I'll help you with that Vein. And when it's done, you'll keep your end of the deal, too."

For a second, he squinted his eyes at me. "Don't you remember what I told you today? I've read about a touched vampire that came looking for my great-great-grandfather's help," he said. "He died when they separated him from his spirit."

Letting go a long breath, I nodded. "But there's a ten percent chance I'll make it, too."

"Yes—*ten* percent," he said. "That's not much."

"It's enough. It's a chance."

"Nikki—that's suicide."

"It's a chance, Jacob. And I'm taking it. You have no choice. You made that oath with me."

He shook his head, looking like I'd just slapped him hard across the face. "Why?" he said. "Is it so bad to be touched when the alternative is *death*?"

"Ninety-percent death," I reminded him.

But he still didn't get it. "Why?"

"Because I want to."

"That's not reason enough."

"Sure, it is."

"It's because you want to mate with him, don't you." It wasn't a question.

"None of your business."

He smiled, but he somehow looked in pain. "You *do* love him."

I raised my brows. "Jealous?"

But the strangest thing, his heart skipped a beat.

He turned away from me, holding his hips. "You would choose a ninety-percent chance of dying over *not* being with him?"

I grinned. "I never said I was smart." Just crazy about a man he considered a monster.

Jumping off the rocks, I dusted off my skirt. It was torn in a few places, but as long as it didn't fall off me completely, I'd put it on. My shirt and jacket didn't make it, though. I still had to put on one of the old shirts Jacob brought me, but at least the skirt was from Ax. "I need some blood and then we can get to training."

Jacob smiled, shaking his head. "You do understand that you can walk away from this, don't you?"

"Yep. I'm choosing not to—but *not* because I'm a good girl, Jacob. It's because I need something from you. Let's not forget that."

I was only a *good girl* when I was with Ax. And if everything went right, I'd be a good girl with him again.

Even when Jacob brought me some cold blood from the fridge, and even after he made his circle in the sand to keep himself safe when I let the spirit out, I still felt uneasy. I still couldn't stop thinking about the way Ax had looked at me in that cave. All that pain and all that rage reflection in his eyes. And his words, too. *Don't bother.* But he already knew me well enough to not expect that of me. And I would bother. I would do anything to be with him, even if he didn't understand it yet.

And if he really meant those words, I would change his mind, even if it took me a lifetime.

Whatever it takes.

—THE END

*Thank you for reading **Damsel in Distress**!*
*I hope you enjoyed the continuation of Nikki and Ax's story. The third and final book in this series, **Deadly Match**, is now available on Amazon!*

For more books, turn the page, or you can follow me on Amazon, social media, or visit www.dnhoxa.com

Sincerely,
Dori Hoxa

More by D.N. Hoxa: The Reign of Dragons Series

King of Air (Reign of Dragons, Book 1)

Being stuck in a time loop sucks, especially when I die on the same day, at the hands of the same man, over and over again. But in Life Number Seven, I'm determined to change my fate.

You'd think being the princess of all shifters would come with benefits and glamour and *freedom*--it doesn't. It comes with isolation, constant fear, and a fabric over my head the whole damn time.

Nobody will believe me or lift a finger to help me figure out why I'm stuck in this loop, not even my father, the dragon king. If I dare to even mention it to him, I end up with a bloody lip. Yeah, he's a very hard man to talk to. That's why I have no other choice but to switch places with my maid and run away.

But things don't exactly go as planned when I'm kidnapped and find myself a captive of my father's sworn enemy. *Just my luck.*

Lucien Di Laurier is a cocky bastard who thinks I'm an object to be owned. It doesn't help that he's impossibly beautiful and can literally control the air in my lungs with a wave of his hand. He wants to get his revenge on the king, and that's why he's after the princess…never realizing that I'm right there, in his home, pretending to be my maid. He vows to break me until I tell him all of my secrets, but…

That still doesn't stop me.

He'll kill me if he finds out my real name. He'll probably do worse things before that, but I can't help myself. He's everything I was never allowed to have. He's blinding light and passion and *life*, the perfect mistake wrapped up in a pretty ribbon, just for me.

So I take what I can get even knowing how it will all end... until it does.

PIXIE PINK SERIES

Werewolves Like Pink Too (Pixie Pink, Book 1)

What's worse than a pink pixie living all alone in the Big City, eight thousand miles away from home?

A pink pixie who's stuck behind a desk all day, taking calls and managing monster-fighting crews without ever seeing the light of day herself. *That's* what.

For two years, I worked my ass off to prove myself to my boss, and prayed for a chance to do the work I left my family behind for.

And I'm finally about to catch my break. I've got an undercover mission with my name on it, and it's everything I've been dreaming of since I got here.

Until I find out that Dominic Dane will be my partner. That self absorbed, narcissistic werewolf who humiliated me in front of all my coworkers on day one, and loves to pretend that I don't even exist.

It's bad enough that he tried to kick me out of my mission. It's even worse that he's sinfully hot and fries braincells with a single look of those gorgeous green eyes.

Now, on top of having to kick ass on my first mission, I have to pretend to be his *girlfriend* for three days, and keep my ridiculous attraction to him under control, too. So much for catching a break.

Lucky for me, I've got a secret weapon that's going to help me handle Dominic Dane, and it's God's best gift to mankind: chocolate. Armed with as many bars as my purse can fit, and with my wits about me, I'm going to survive the gorgeous wolf-ass one way or the other—and *win*.

THE NEW YORK SHADE SERIES

Magic Thief (The New York Shade, Book 1)

Welcome to the New York Shade!

My name is Sin Montero--hellbeast mercenary, professional liar, and I'll happily be your guide.

Supernaturals are free to be who they are in the Shade. That's the point of its existence--just not for me. I've spent my whole life lying about what I am, until it all comes crashing down on me with a single bite. Turns out, my blood can't tell lies, not to a vampire.

Damian Reed is achingly beautiful the way a lion is breathtaking--right until he rips your throat out. He claims my baby brother is in trouble...

THE NEW ORLEANS SHADE SERIES

Pain Seeker (The New Orleans Shade, Book 1)

Betrayed. Defeated. Chained.

I used to be a sister, a friend, a ruler of the elflands that belonged to my family's House. Now, I am a prisoner of the fae, my kind's sworn enemy since the beginning of time.

They put chains around me, thinking they can keep me from breaking free and taking their lives. They can't.

The only reason I stay is because I no longer need a life. My home, my family, my dignity were all taken away from me.

But I have the fae. My captor. He is every bit the man I was taught to hate long before I knew how to love...

THE DARK SHADE SERIES

Shadow Born (The Dark Shade, Book 1)

They call me Kallista Nix, but that is not my real name. *My past was taken from me, and though I search for it every day for the past five years, all I find are dead ends.*

Though I search for the Dark Shade, everyone keeps telling me that it doesn't exist. The darkness, the monsters, the fear—they're all in my head. I'm tempted to believe them. The Shades are magical safe havens where everyone can be who they truly are without having to hide. Supernaturals of all kinds love them. They're not supposed to be *dark*. But how can I argue with my own memories? Everything changes when I steal a magical artifact…

SMOKE & ASHES SERIES

Firestorm (Smoke & Ashes, Book 1)

Having no soul definitely has its perks.

After all, I can kill as many magical beasts as I want and not have to worry about the blood on my hands. But no matter how hard I try to run, I can never escape where I came from: the pits of Hell. Now Hell's elite have a job for me, a job I can't refuse. A nocturnal witch is on the loose and those are never up to anything good. She's hiding in my city, so they've decided I'm the best person for the job—together with Lexar Dagon'an. He's Hell's very own Golden Boy, my archnemesis, and he's sexy as the sins he makes me want to commit when I look at him. Like *murder*, obviously...

ALSO BY D.N. HOXA

Winter Wayne Series (Completed)

Bone Witch

Bone Coven

Bone Magic

Bone Spell

Bone Prison

Bone Fairy

Scarlet Jones Series (Completed)

Storm Witch

Storm Power

Storm Legacy

Storm Secrets

Storm Vengeance

Storm Dragon

Victoria Brigham Series (Completed)

Wolf Witch

Wolf Uncovered

Wolf Unleashed

Wolf's Rise

The Marked Series (Completed)

Blood and Fire

Deadly Secrets

Death Marked

Starlight Series (Completed)

Assassin

Villain

Sinner

Savior

Morta Fox Series (Completed)

Heartbeat

Reclaimed

Unchanged

Printed in Great Britain
by Amazon